HOW
the
HANGMAN
LOST *His*
HEART

Liam

HOW the HANGMAN LOST His HEART

K. M. GRANT

SCHOLASTIC INC.

New York Toronto London Auckland Sydney
Mexico City New Delhi Hong Kong Buenos Aires

ISBN-13: 978-0-545-08070-5
ISBN-10: 0-545-08070-3

12 11 10 9 8 7 6 5 4 3 2 1   8 9 10 11 12 13/0

Printed in the U.S.A.   40

First Scholastic printing, January 2008

Book designed and typeset by Yelena Safronova

In memory of all the nice hangmen in history
who kept their hands always steady
and their steel always sharp.

It was a horrid job, but somebody had to do it.

Acknowledgments

I would like to thank all the children who, having heard me speak of the hapless head of Uncle Frank, encouraged me to write this story.

I would also like to apologize to Uncle Frank himself, for digging him up, as it were, yet again.

Sorry, Uncle Frank.

HOW the HANGMAN LOST His HEART

London, August 10, 1746

When Uncle Frank's head was finally parted from his body, the crowd laughed. It was not nice laughter, the sort that gurgles up when you are happy or have just played a trick. This laughter was the kind you hear in a bad dream and Alice, standing in the crowd, wanted to thump those around her who joined in. It was quite the wrong time for laughter. It was true that her uncle had laughed himself as he was carted over Kennington Common, even though, what with the rope around his neck and his hands bound behind him, his laughter was scratchy as burned toast. Still, it was admirable under the circumstances that he laughed at all. Why, he had even managed to tell a joke! It was not a very good joke, to be sure, and perhaps the funniest thing about it was his face when he couldn't remember the punch line. "What a moment for a memory lapse," he had cried gaily. "The joke's on me!" But that was before. When the executioner had produced the grisly tools of his trade, Uncle Frank had turned green.

Everybody knew that the punch line would never come now.

Alice had not been able to watch after that, but the sighs and appalled groans of the crowd gave an up-to-the-minute commentary as her beloved uncle was first strung up, then cut down before he was dead, sliced open like a halibut or perhaps a herring, and had his innards removed. Only then was he relieved of his suffering and his head. That was when the laughter came and Alice was violently sick all over somebody's shoes. She did not apologize. She was too busy wiping her mouth carefully on her skirt and stiffening her backbone. It would not do to look fainthearted when she went to claim the body.

Dan Skinslicer, hangman and jobbing executioner (prices on request: any method considered), was not an unkindly soul and when he saw Alice, who couldn't help trembling as she approached the gallows, he rubbed his hands on his breeches before showing her the coffin into which Uncle Frank's remains had been tossed. "You here for Colonel Towneley?" he asked, thinking to pat her shoulder, then, seeing that Uncle Frank's blood was leaking from under his fingernails, just nodding at her instead. "The innards are not there," he said sympathetically, taking off his stained apron. "We burn them, see. The fire's behind the scaffold. Just

2

a small one today, with only the colonel and one or two others to do. Now, have you brought a cart?"

Alice steadied herself. "I ordered a boy to bring one," she said, finding it hard not to look inside the coffin although she didn't want to. "I gave him sixpence, but he's late. Can you wait?"

Dan wanted his dinner, but Alice looked at him with such pleading in her eyes that he found himself nodding and they sat together on the steps of the scaffold as the usual execution-day caterwauling and chaos died away and the last of the nasty jeering boys had spat at Uncle Frank and run away.

Dan leaned over and wiped the gobs carefully off with his apron. "There's no call for that kind of thing," he said reprovingly. "The colonel may have wanted airy-fairy Charlie Stuart on the throne of England instead of our nice King George, but he was a gentleman and he gave me a very decent tip."

"Can't we put the coffin lid on?" asked Alice plaintively. She felt faint and shivery. She had not even paused to pick up a shawl as she ran from her grandmother's house that morning in case somebody saw her and stopped her from getting out at all. Her aunt Ursula thought it much too dangerous for any of the family to witness Uncle Frank's final disgrace and had spent the whole evening clutching her own throat theatrically as if it was she who was facing execution.

By the end, Alice had wanted to strangle her. Stupid Aunt Ursula! *She* was perfectly safe. No self-respecting executioner would ever want to swipe through a neck as scraggy as hers.

The wooden steps creaked as Dan sat down, his legs two solid logs in front of him. He found an apple in his pocket, inspected it, and rubbed at the blood spatters. "Bite?" he offered. Alice made a revolted face and he shrugged. "I haven't had any breakfast yet," he told her, basking in the feeling of a job well done. "Never do, somehow, on execution mornings, although I make sure the wife gives me a good dinner after. Mutton pie tonight."

Another gob of spit landed on Uncle Frank. A latecomer had missed the execution but wasn't going to be done out of all the fun.

"Please," begged Alice, "please can we put the coffin lid on?"

"I'm sorry, but we can't," Dan told her with his mouth full. Clearly Alice had a lot to learn about executions. "I'm waiting for instructions from old Pecksy about his head."

Alice swayed and shut her eyes. She had forgotten, or perhaps just did not want to remember, what they might decide to do to her uncle's head. When she opened her eyes again, six soldiers were clearing a path for Lord Chief Justice Peckersniff.

The Lord Chief Justice didn't waste any time. He dismounted with a dainty flourish and tiptoed up the scaffold steps. "Good job, Skinslicer," he said, carefully covering his nose and mouth with his handkerchief before peering in at Uncle Frank. "Got the pitch pot handy?"

"Here, sir," said Dan.

"Well, stick Colonel Towneley's noggin in it and give him a good dunking. We don't want him falling to bits. His head must be up on Temple Bar tonight and be on display for quite some time as a lesson, Skinslicer, as a lesson I say to all other traitors. We want no more of his sort, I say no more. Now be sharp. I've promised my wife that she can come for a viewing before we have our dinner. She always enjoys your executions, Skinslicer. She only missed today's because she was having new teeth fitted." He tried not to let his nose twitch, but the memory of Lady Peckersniff's rotting gums made him feel queasier than Uncle Frank's corpse. He looked about for something more uplifting and spotted Alice. He had no idea who she was, but, from the lofty height of his important position, he liked to be kind to those he thought of as "the little people." He gave Dan an awkward wink and asked, "Who is your apprentice?"

Outraged, Alice shot up, but Dan pushed her back down. Silly child! Did she not know that being a

.or's niece was hardly something to be advertised?
. smiled, showing one yellow incisor. "She's my sister's girl," he said. "She came to give me this." He held out his apple. Despite Dan's best efforts, Uncle Frank's blood had stained it pink all the way through.

This was not good for Peckersniff's delicate stomach and he rose on his tiptoes and retreated rapidly. Only once settled back in the saddle did he twist his lips into a smile. Always, always keep on good terms with the hangman, his old father had told him, because you never know when he might come for *you*. In these uncertain days, it was best to lay it on thick as mustard. He glanced quickly at Uncle Frank. "Marvelous work, marvelous work, Skinslicer. Such neat slicing! Such tidy chopping! The king—the real king rather than any pretendy one—will be most impressed, I say most impressed." He flapped his hand, then placed his handkerchief firmly back over his nose before cantering away. Oh my, but the smell of the common people was really something awful.

When he was safely out of sight, Dan was very apologetic. "Sorry, missy," he said to Alice, "but it wouldn't do to say you were with the colonel. He's a bit unpredictable, that Justice Peckersniff. The good news is that he only wants your uncle's head, so you'll get a whole body to take home, which is nice. Sometimes traitors are hacked into four bits, you know, and sent off to different towns. I saw a beautiful leg in Bath last year. Executioner'd done a fine job. It stank a bit and was an odd shade of purple, mind, but you could see the cut was quite clean. Don't know who the hangman was, but that leg had the mark of a real sawbones about it." He threw his apple away, jumped down, and chose a pike from a bundle lying under the gallows. "Now, turn round while I do what has to be done."

After some scraping and a bit of swearing, Dan said, "You can look now," and there was Uncle Frank with the top of the pike poking out of his skull. Alice thought she might be sick again, but luckily she wasn't. Dan himself spat on a bit of cloth and washed Uncle Frank's face with it. "If you want to make yourself useful," he said, "you can rearrange the colonel's hair. I don't expect he'd like to look a mess." Not wanting to be thought unhelpful, Alice obeyed. The hair was difficult to manage, what with being covered in pitch and all, but she did her best and by the time she and Dan had finished, Uncle Frank was really quite presentable. His handsome face had certainly been a little altered by Dan's ax: it was thinner and he looked older than he had only moments before, but at least he was still recognizably Uncle Frank and seemed, under the circumstances, quite pleased.

Alice at once felt better. "You have every reason to be pleased," she muttered as she made final adjustments to his globby locks. It felt odd to be addressing a dis-embodied head, but not as odd as she thought it might. "Not many could have endured a martyrdom like that without moaning or screaming or peeing in their breeches."

It was only when they had finished that Dan stared at Frank with some consternation.

"What?" asked Alice, looking nervously back and forth from Uncle Frank to Dan. "What is it?"

"Well," said Dan, scratching his head and leaving a lump of pitch on his fringe, "it's just that most of the gentlemen I execute shut their eyes. Your uncle Frank has kept his open. He's looking at us. I've never seen that before. It's a bit spooky, to be honest."

"Well, he's quite dead," said Alice tartly, and suddenly she found she was blinking back tears. There had been nobody else in Alice's life quite like Uncle Frank. He had slipped her silver, let her ride his horse, and, unbeknownst to her parents, on his last visit to her home at Towneley Hall had taken her to see a prize fight between two greased men in the market square at Withinby. How badly she had wanted to go with him when he set off to join Bonnie Prince Charlie. How she had begged. How cross she had been when he declared that her pretty face would only distract men from their proper duty of killing each other. But how she shuddered now, as the smoke from the smoldering innards stung her nostrils. Imagine if the innards were hers! Imagine if—

She was saved from too much imagining by a piping voice coming from below. "Wagon for Uncle Frank?" the diminutive driver asked, tilting a mop of curly hair above a freckly face. "Sixpence paid, another sixpence to come."

"Goodness," thought Alice, for the boy could not have been more than nine. Dan was already hammering down the coffin lid, so Alice held the pike. She had to use both hands, for Uncle Frank's head was heavier than she expected and the pike swayed dangerously.

"Now," said the boy, "pile in. You, missy, can sit atop the dead man's box, unless you think your old captain too sniffy for that kind of caper."

"He was a *colonel*, if you don't mind," said Alice, suddenly prim.

The boy snorted.

Half an hour later, Alice, Dan, the cart boy, the coffin, and Uncle Frank's head were being pelted with squelchy vegetables as they trundled through the narrow, dank streets toward the river. Some of the rude words that accompanied the vegetables made Dan's eyebrows shoot so far up they disappeared and, although the pony skittered along as fast as he could go, it seemed an age to Alice before they reached the great stone arches of Christopher Wren's Temple Bar.

As they drew up underneath, she didn't know whether to be relieved or horrified. Several heads were already displayed on spikes high above the coping that spanned the road and, although the erstwhile owners of the heads were unknown to her, she felt outraged at the indignity of it all.

She grabbed Dan. "Don't put Uncle Frank's head up there. I can't bear it."

"Ouch, missy," said Dan, for Alice's fingernails were sharp. "I must. That's my job, see." He shook the pike to get the head straight. "It's all right for rich people like you"—he wiped some brown mush that might once have been potato off the end of Uncle Frank's nose—"but if I don't work, me and my missus will starve. They might even send me on to the ships." His grimy cheeks went white at the thought because he had once executed a cabin boy whose innards were so slimy they wouldn't even burn. "I couldn't do that."

"But my family would pay you," pleaded Alice.

"I'm sorry," said Dan. He took a firm hold of the pike. "I wouldn't look if I were you."

But Alice could not look anywhere else. With awful fascination she watched as Dan got out of the cart, fought his way through the hustlers and jostlers, and, negotiating the length of the pike as best he could, disappeared into the shop that provided the only access to the top of the monument. Eventually he reappeared dragging a ladder and climbed up, over the great stone scrolls and onto the roof. Conscious of Alice staring up from below, he did some last-minute tidying of Uncle Frank's hair before raising the head high and easing the pike into its hole, where it wobbled a little before coming to rest. Ever the professional, he couldn't help taking a quick glance at Uncle Frank's unknown neighbor, whose neck, unlike Uncle Frank's, was a real mess. *Honest to God*, Dan thought as he made his way back down to the street, *some people take no pride in their work.*

As he climbed into the cart the clouds thickened and even the hardiest onlookers felt the carnival spirit of the morning evaporating fast. When it started to drizzle, it was clear that the fun was over. Alice's teeth began to chatter, but she would do her duty, just as Uncle Frank would expect. "B-b-b-b-boy," she commanded, "take Mr. S-s-s-skinslicer home first, then drop me and what's left of Uncle Frank at my granny's. Somebody else will take his p-p-p-poor body home."

The boy made a horrible face. "Hope home's not far," he said.

"About 250 miles to the north," Alice told him.

The boy burped. "He'll pong summat terrible by the time he gets there."

Alice thought she had never felt sick so many times in one day before.

The boy clicked to the pony and Alice looked up one last time. She could not help exclaiming at what she saw. The drizzle, persistent now, made it look as though her uncle was crying. "Of course, it's just the raindrops," she told herself sternly. "I know it's just the raindrops." Nevertheless, she hated to leave him looking so dismal and, unable to restrain herself any longer, burst into just the kind of loud and noisy sobs that she prided herself she had quite grown out of.

It was not until early afternoon that the pony drew up wearily in front of the solid stone house in Grosvenor Square that belonged to Lady Widdrington, Alice's grandmother. Alice climbed stiffly over the side and paid the boy more than the sixpence she had promised, for it had been a thoroughly unpleasant journey. Dan lived on the side of what Alice could only describe as a drain. There Johanna, his brassy wife, had been waiting for him, swinging a pail of slops as greasy as her skin. "Papists! I can smell 'em!" she had screamed, and had tipped the slops all down the poor pony's hind legs, where great lumps had stuck.

Alice had pretended Johanna did not exist and just thanked Dan for his work, telling him, in a precise voice that quavered only occasionally, that if anybody had had to execute Uncle Frank, she was glad it had been him. Her gratitude and her handshake had made Dan blush. That made Johanna scream louder than ever.

Once back in Grosvenor Square, however, Alice forgot about Dan and seized the heavy iron latch, calling for help. The house was in pitch darkness, for Aunt Ursula had been too nervous to light the lamps, and it was some time before a light bobbed down the stairs. To take her mind off her brother-in-law's execution, Ursula had been tying pink-and-green ribbons in her bright yellow wig and the effect was, to say the least, unfortunate. When she saw Alice, she started and her ribbons trembled. "Oh, Alice, Alice," she cried, blinking her eyes. "Your grandmother will be relieved to see you. Where *have* you been?" Then she spotted the cart boy. "And who on earth is this?"

"Where do you think I've been?" Alice replied sharply. The sight of her aunt always fired her temper. "I've been to see Uncle Frank chopped up, Aunt, as you well know. And if you had as many guts as Uncle Frank—although, of course, he doesn't have any now—but if you had had half of what he once had, if you see what I mean, you would have been there too. He was always so nice to you."

"And so troublesome too, I'll have you remember, young lady, with his fancy French songs and his naughty ways." Ursula's lips thinned into cheese wires but her eyelashes fluttered as she remembered how Frank had tickled her. Oh, who would tickle her now?

"Well," Alice said, finding her aunt's expression disturbing, "he's going to cause a bit more trouble yet. We've got his coffin outside."

Ursula gave a shriek. "You've brought the body of a traitor here? Get away with you, Alice. Do you want us all taken to the Tower?"

"Oh, pish!" said Alice crisply, deliberately using a word forbidden by her parents. "Uncle Frank is—was— no traitor. Any anyway, Aunt, we haven't brought all of him here. His head's up on Temple Bar. Nobody will know whose body this is. It could be yours—well, almost." Alice's knowledge of male anatomy was more advanced than her family ever suspected.

"Oh, just get it out, get it out!" Ursula clacked her heels. She knew nothing about male anatomy at all. "We can't get it out because it's not in," said the boy, who was enjoying himself. This woman—if that is what she really was—should be in the circus!

Alice glared and wasted no more time before calling for Bunion the coachman and the pantry boys to set Uncle Frank's coffin on the dining table. No sooner had they plonked the coffin down when a tiny old woman, bent and wizened as an ancient spring onion, tottered down the stairs, her face almost hidden by a wig that dwarfed even Ursula's. As an additional, if unintentional, decoration, she was covered, from head to toe, in blue wig powder.

"Hello, hello," she growled, for her once sweet voice had lurched downward with each passing birthday and now, so old she had lost count, was almost in her goatskin boots. "What's going on?"

Alice and her aunt exchanged glances. Granny must be in one of her really forgetful moods not to remember Frank's execution. Alice braved the blue clouds and moved to kiss Lady Widdrington's papery cheek. "She's not going to mind Uncle Frank's body being here," she hissed as she brushed past Ursula, "because she's not even going to remember who Uncle Frank is—was."

"All the more reason to get him away," Ursula hissed back, her wig wobbling like a bird's nest in the wind.

"All in good time. But his body has to wait somewhere." Alice itched to pull Ursula's wig right off. Her grandmother was peering sideways at the cart boy. Was this one of her children? She put out a claw and the boy backed into the corner. Alice took the claw instead. "Granny," she coaxed in a voice of honeyed innocence, "can Uncle Frank stay here just for the night?"

The old lady looked puzzled. "Frank, Frank," she murmured, her face crumpling like a raisin. Then she perked up. "Frank!" she said. "Frank! What a fool I am! Of course he can, my turtledove. Does he need somewhere to lay his pretty head?"

"Not exactly, Granny, but he does need somewhere to lie down."

"Well, we've plenty of space," came the reply. "We could lay a mattress on the table here if this dirty box wasn't taking up so much room." Lady Widdrington gave the coffin a vicious poke.

"That's all right, Granny," said Alice hastily. "We'll find somewhere."

The old lady glared at Ursula. "Go and tell the servants to shift themselves. Frank's coming. He likes good food and the more you feed him, the more wicked he is. It's all humbug, I know, but still, he's one of the few pleasures I have left. Not that you care about my pleasures, Ursula. Look at you. All those ribbons can't hide the fact that you're forty and a spinster and bring me no pleasure at all." She winked secretively at Alice. "How did I produce such a twiggy specimen? I blame Ursula's father, you know. As for *your* father, Alice deary, I'd certainly have run off with him if he'd asked, but he wanted your mother instead, the booby. Now, I'm going upstairs to put on a good dress and some more powder. I suggest you do the same. Maybe Uncle Frank will bring a friend and it is high time, Alice my lovely, that you thought about marriage or you may end up like *her*." She pointed dismissively at Ursula. "We'll dine at five."

Alice cast a glance half-triumphant and half-sympathetic at her aunt. In an act of small rebellion, Ursula stuck out her tongue before snapping off down the passage. She was thirty-eight, not forty, as her mother very well knew, and she had her admirers, or would have if only her mother didn't frighten them all away.

"I'll be off now," said the cart boy. He was glad his mother was just a plain old drunk who beat him. At least she hugged him afterward. You couldn't imagine Lady Widdrington hugging anybody, and as for that Ursula, you'd need paying before hugging her.

Alice showed him out. "Thank you," she said. "I'm sorry about Dan's wife throwing those slops at the pony. He's a nice pony too."

"Never mind," said the boy, giving Alice a friendly dig in the ribs. "It'll wash off. And if ever you're in the same position as your uncle Frank, I'll come and help give you a good send-off."

Alice watched him go in silence.

When five o'clock came, Lady Widdrington did not appear and, unable to bear the thought of dining alone with Ursula, Alice took herself off to bed. She could hear the rain beginning to beat down. What a dreadful time to be alive, she thought as she huddled into a tiny ball and watched the candle flame flicker. Who cared who was king? She only cared that she would never hear Uncle Frank's teasing voice or be swept into his welcoming arms again. He was the reason she had agreed to come to London in the first place. She hadn't wanted to. The thought of staying with Faraway Granny, as they called Lady Widdrington, was distinctly unappealing. But Uncle Frank had whirled her around and told her how he would take her to coffeehouses and the theater and how she should have a smart London horse and they would ride at Kew together. He had laid out a life of such unimaginable glamour and sophistication, in which he had promised that she would be the star, that Alice's reluctance had melted away. With Uncle Frank's promises ringing in her head, she had said good-bye to her mother and her old nurse with barely a qualm and, indeed, had been filled with the happiest anticipation.

Then came the rebellion and everything went wrong. Uncle Frank vanished *and* on the back of the beautiful horse he had bought her, something for which she still couldn't quite forgive him. Worse, everybody was so nervous, hardly daring to swallow in case it reminded others that there were still throats waiting to be cut, that fun was in short supply. Even now, with the rebellion ended, life would hardly be the same without Uncle Frank. What was left except listening to Aunt Ursula's gripes during the day and endless evenings powdering Granny's monstrous hairpieces?

She rolled over. Grosvenor Square was finished for her. It was time to go home. What wouldn't she give to find herself, at this moment, in the orchard being licked by the dogs, with her father stroking his knuckles and droning on, as he always did, about how to measure rainfall. Never again would she be bored by his notebooks and colored graphs. Never again would she surreptitiously empty the contents of his chamber pot into his scientifically placed glass jars. And never again would she agree to come to London.

A crash on the front door made her jump. Bunion was shouting and, for a moment, Alice wondered if they were being attacked by a mob. But it was only the wagoner come to collect the coffin. Alice splashed some water from her ewer onto her face, then ran downstairs and outside. Maybe she could go home in the hearse. The wagoner was certainly willing. "You can come if you want, missy," he said, looking her up and down and smiling in a knowing way. "You'll be warmer company during the night than a headless corpse."

Alice froze, but not with fear. Oh, lordy me! Uncle Frank's head! She had not been thinking straight. How could she leave London with it still up on Temple Bar? She couldn't! Uncle Frank would think she had entirely deserted him.

She drew herself up to her full height, which was considerably more than the wagoner's. "That's my uncle Frank you are talking about," she said imperiously, "and whether I come with you or not, if you don't treat him with respect, he'll haunt you. Do you know about haunting? Well, let me tell you that Uncle Frank, headless or not, died with *his eyes open.*" She very slowly raised one eyebrow, then the other, an old trick she had often used to frighten her nurse. "That means he sees everything, *everything,* and if you don't deliver him safely, your own head will rot and *drop off of its own accord.*"

The wagoner fled to the top of his box. "You coming then?" he asked nervously. Alice shook her head. The wagoner picked up his whip and immediately the horse raised his tail and let fly a gust of noisy wind. Alice clenched her fists. It was not a glamorous end for Uncle Frank.

As soon as the coffin was out of sight, Ursula peeped out. "Are they gone?" Her face shone white, for she had painted it with zinc in the mistaken belief that it recaptured her youthful bloom. If King George's soldiers did come to arrest them because of their connection with Uncle Frank, maybe one would fall in love with her and she would be saved. Alice slid past her. What did she care for Aunt Ursula? All she could see as she made her way back upstairs was Uncle Frank's head sitting in soggy splendor on Temple Bar, tears running down his pitchy cheeks. She got into bed again, but though she tried, she couldn't sleep. Instead she lay for hours listening to the watchmen shouting to each other and the dogs barking at their shadows. In truth, she wondered how she would ever sleep again with Uncle Frank's head and body in two different places. Indeed, so long as his head was displayed in such a shameful way, how could *anybody* who loved him ever rest? She tossed and turned, then, as she listened to the church bell solemnly strike three, a thought made her go quite rigid. *Perhaps the reason Uncle Frank's eyes wouldn't close was because he was uncomfortable too. Maybe they would only close when he was all back together, head and body, in one place.* Alice clutched at her pillow and slowly, in the dark, a resolution began to form in her mind, a resolution so grim that she wondered if she would ever be able to stick to it. She told herself it was stupid. She told herself it was impossible. But within five minutes, she knew what she was going to do. She was going to steal Uncle Frank's head and get it home herself.

Now she did not even pretend to rest, but got up and began to walk about her room. Faster and faster she paced, as if winding herself up to the right speed, then she ran to her wardrobe to find suitable clothes. *Uncle Frank will not spend one more night on that Temple Bar,* she vowed as she rummaged among her garments, *not one more night.* She pulled out a pink dress, then rejected it because it was too frilly and stealing a head was a serious business—and anyway, she didn't think it suited her and on such an expedition you never knew whom you might meet. In the end she chose a green gown that had once been her best but was now a little battered. That would do very well. She thought her courage was high until she sat down to lace her boots. Then she paused. Now that she was out of it, her bed looked irresistibly downy and inviting. Perhaps she should just get back in. After all, Uncle Frank was dead.

The trouble was that she could see his expression as clearly as if he was in the same room and his open eyes reproached her. Resolutely, she hugged her cloak around her shoulders, took her candle, and tiptoed downstairs. On her way through the hall, being a practical girl, she shoveled up all the money her grandmother kept in the long case clock. Then she quietly let herself out of the back door and, before she could talk herself out of it, hurried away.

It was much longer after dawn than Alice had hoped before she was standing once again underneath Temple Bar. Several times she had lost her bearings and, with the heads now silhouetted against a brightening sky, she needed every ounce of her determination to keep going. The Bar looked so big and she felt so small. She spoke sternly to herself. Having got this far, she would not slink away.

Her first challenge was to get to the top of the monument and to do this she first tried the door of the shop whose staircase Dan had used. Unsurprisingly, it was firmly closed. She glanced up. Uncle Frank glanced down. *Come on,* he seemed to be saying, *come on.* Alice could feel panic creeping pox-like over her skin, because even as she stood there the city was beginning to wake and early traders were already splashing their way through the oily skim left by the rain. Soon the road would be busy. She looked wildly about her.

Amid a mass of building work and scaffolding farther down the street, she spied a long ladder and her spirits rose. Surely that would get her onto the wide ledge parallel to the shop window and, once up there, she was sure she would find the shorter ladder Dan had used to shin up past the scrolls and onto the roof. She craned her neck to see Uncle Frank again. He was still staring straight at her. She steadied herself. She couldn't—wouldn't—disappoint him.

Setting her chin, she ran to the ladder and tilted it over. It was so heavy that she could only just drag it through the wagons collecting the night soil. The tradeshorses stamped their feet as she began to talk aloud to herself. "Keep your head," she repeated again and again, but could not manage even the smallest smile at her joke.

When she finally got the ladder to the Bar, it took her several goes to hook it up against the wall, but eventually, though it threatened occasionally to fall and flatten her, she managed to make it reasonably secure. There was no time to look at Uncle Frank again. Now she must climb.

Nobody took much notice to start with except a few rude chimney sweeps' boys and flower girls. They scoffed but let her be. They saw stranger things than Alice every day. However, after a while, when people began to emerge from their breakfasts, they gathered in small crowds until it seemed as though the entire neighborhood had assembled to watch her progress.

Concentrating hard and counting every rung, Alice climbed higher and higher, higher than the postern gate, higher than the windows, higher than she had ever been before, even when she had climbed the ancient Towneley Hall chestnut tree on a dare. The ladder, once so heavy, seemed flimsier and flimsier, as if the tiniest movement could send it flying and leave her stranded. Her ankles went all rubbery. She closed her eyes and just kept climbing until the rungs gave out. Then she took a deep breath and hauled herself onto the ledge on which the scrolls of the Bar rested. The smaller ladder, as she had thought, was still propped against the buttress and Alice was soon halfway up this too. Then, almost disastrously, she wavered, for although she had the ledge below her, she was suddenly and acutely aware how far above the street she was. Too far. But it was no good going all wobbly now, just when she had to work out exactly how to remove the head from the pike. In Grosvenor Square, this had seemed like a minor detail. Now it seemed easier to knit with rats' tails. Nevertheless, she must try.

Once on the roof itself, Alice flattened herself out and began to crawl over the curved lead. It was slippery and as soon as the pike was within grasping distance she grabbed it thankfully. However, to her horror, her grabbing made Uncle Frank's head spin around. "Stay still, Uncle Frank! Stay still," she cried. After a long minute, both head and pike stopped twirling and Alice managed to haul herself up the pike shaft, one hand above the other. Pushing her feet against a ridge, with great difficulty she began to pull the pike shaft out. It swayed like a drunk.

A veritable age later, she felt a lurch and the pike suddenly came loose. But now, horrors! Though she tried to be so careful, Alice was not strong enough to hold it and it crashed off the roof and onto the ledge. There was a loud crack as Uncle Frank's nose hit the scroll, but since this was nothing in comparison with what he had endured already, Alice did not waste time apologizing but saved what remained of her energy to clamber down in pursuit.

Yet now that Uncle Frank's head was within reach, how hard it was to approach! Alice loved Uncle Frank, she really did. But he certainly seemed different without his body attached. Her movements became very tentative. First she took off her cloak and laid it out. Then, screwing her eyes as tightly shut as she could without blotting out all her vision, she dropped to her hands and knees, crawled to the end of the pike, seized Uncle Frank's hair, and, with a desperate tug, jerked his head free. This was much worse, much

much worse, than any nightmare. It took every ounce of her courage to crawl back to her cloak and wrap the head up in it, because—and this was something Alice had not bargained for—it was impossible to avoid being spotted with blood and other stuff quite unmentionable. *Never again,* she swore to herself as she turned her cloak into a makeshift sack, tied a knot in it, and hooked it over her arm for her descent. *Never, ever again.*

The descent should have been easier, only it wasn't because Alice's whole body rattled as if she had the palsy. "Help me, Uncle Frank," she prayed. But how could he help her, when all that was left of him was his silent stare and a pair of pale lips? By the time she got back to the ladder, her shoes were so slippery and her muscles so achy that several times, as she eased herself onto the top rung, she missed her footing and nearly fell. It was no good telling herself not to be so silly, that all she had to do was climb down the way she'd gotten up. When you are clutching a head, things don't appear quite that simple.

The crowd had fallen silent as soon as they realized what this strange little figure was doing. Now they watched with growing disbelief. Some began to mutter and shake their heads. Others backed away. They wanted to see if Alice made it to the ground, but even to witness such an audacious theft of a criminal's head was an act of treason toward the king. They remained only because they were gripped by an atmosphere tense as a breaking thunderstorm.

But it was not thunder they heard. Quite suddenly, the air was filled with the brisk clatter of hooves and, above it, a voice shouting, "Move. Move for Kingston's Light Horse! Make way."

Alice, at last firmly established on the long ladder and beginning to feel as if she had made it, choked. Not soldiers, surely not soldiers? Please, please let them just pass on.

They did not. Instead, there was a barked order to stop and her head swam as she saw dozens of shiny boots and dozens of open mouths tilted up toward her. "Ignore them. Ignore them," she ordered herself. But it was no good. Her concentration was broken and, with Uncle Frank a dead weight at her side, all she could imagine now was spiraling down, her hair streaming like a great yellow wave. She clutched at the ladder rungs, her ears full of the jangling of steel bits and the occasional impatient rasp of iron-shod hoof against cobble. These sounds were not reassuring.

Forcing her eyes to focus, she began to climb onto the ledge again. Maybe escape was possible over the rooftops. But from out of high windows, people were leaning forward, anxious, so it seemed to Alice, not to help her but to arrest her. One man actually had his leg over the sill and when Alice heard him drop down behind her, she grabbed the short ladder and began to climb back onto the roof. Oh, why was Uncle Frank's head so heavy? She could hear the man's excited panting. He would get her! He would get her!

Practically without thinking, she did the only thing she could. She hauled herself from the ladder not onto the roof but onto the cornice that ran above the frieze of the Bar. Clinging to the coping as far as its slope permitted, she edged her way along, facing inward toward the ashlar stones. She moved very slowly, her hands feeling their way, for the surface was rough and chipped in places and to balance she had to press her weight hard onto the balls of her feet. The cornice was terrifyingly narrow and Uncle Frank unbalanced her. Nevertheless, it worked. Her pursuer did not follow but, laughing, gave the short ladder a hefty push and sent it sliding away.

Alice hardly had time to take this in before a breeze caught the bottom of her dress and it billowed out like a sail. She would be torn away! But at the last moment the breeze was kind and changed direction. Now it slammed her against the pediment and squashed her chin in some bird droppings. Far below, the crowd oohed and aahed, but Alice did not hear them. All she knew now was that if the wind blew again and swung Uncle Frank's head just a little harder, she would fall and die. She forced herself to ease her bundle off her arm and onto the cornice beside her. She still had to hold it, which left only one arm with which to steady herself against the stone, but at least she felt more stable. After a short rest, she began to ease herself and her precious cargo carefully along until, in the middle of the pediment, she stopped. Too late, she realized that climbing onto the cornice was the stupidest thing she could have done. The coping arched and she was too short to reach its fullest height, so she could not get over to the other side. She would be here forever, or at least until her raised arm ached so much that it could no longer support her. She would have cried, except that tears seemed far too feeble a response.

Underneath the main arch, a stony-faced dragoon major dismounted from his horse and stood, apparently deep in contemplation. Years ago he had been a good-looking man, but too many military campaigns had coarsened his face, and eyes that might once have been kindly had long since turned sour. Looking up at Alice, he did not see a girl, he saw another traitor—there were a lot around these days. True, he had come across this one by chance, as he and his men accompanied a thief to the gallows, but he would see justice done, you see if he didn't. He watched Alice almost nonchalantly, flicking imaginary dust from his yellow cuffs. When she swayed this way and that and the crowd sighed, half-hoping and half-dreading that this fair-headed heroine would end up a bloodied pulp in the gutter, he shifted his legs a little wider apart. He was in no hurry. Executions were two a penny, but a pretty prisoner was a rarity. When he had secured Alice, he would take her to the barracks and, after suitable questioning, which might or might not involve a little physical "discomfort," he would hand her over to the authorities with a confession hung around her neck. His lips curled in what passed for a smile. His men, milling about on their uniformly black and bobtailed horses, saw the curl and felt sorry for Alice. It was their experience that recipients of such a curl seldom survived long. Sensing their sympathy, the major clapped his heels together and barked at them. "Back into your lines, you fish-eyed fleabags!" The reaction was gratifyingly electric. Even the horses jumped. "Captain Ffrench!" He turned on his second-in-command. "Are you a soldier or a lapdog? These men are not children on a nursery outing. You forget your duty, sir."

The captain on his handsome gelding had been helping the cornet, who usually held only the troop's colors, hold on to the major's horse—for the cornet was small and the animal strong. Now he let go and began to shout orders himself. "Form back into your riding order," he cried. "I'll see two lines. Come on now, troopers. No more gawping at the lady."

The major settled his legs apart again. "So you think she's a lady, do you, Captain Ffrench?"

"Well, sir." Hew Ffrench's voice betrayed his nerves. He had once loved the army, but life under Major Slavering needed a stronger constitution than he possessed. "She's certainly a female."

The troopers laughed and the major's eyes narrowed. Two vertical dents appeared as he sucked in his cheeks. The laughter died away. Hew tensed. He knew those dents.

"Get off your horse." Every word was enunciated clearly. The crowd shushed at each other and shimmied forward. Here was more sport. What a day this was turning into.

"Now," said the major, stroking his mustache, "where are your manners, Captain Ffrench? Up on the Bar, as you have noted, we have a 'lady' in distress. But tell me this. What is the point of having two fs in your name if, having identified a 'lady,' you can't behave as a man with two fs should?" Now the major turned to the people, inviting them to appreciate his humor. They obliged. "Shall we send him up after the blond damsel, my good friends? Shall we order Captain

Ffffffrench up the ladder and along the ledge to get our lady traitor?"

"Yes! Yes! Send him up! Send him up!" went the cry. The crowd felt much more at ease now.

Hew stood his ground. "You know that I cannot stand heights," he said pleasantly enough, even laughing a little to give the major every opportunity to include him in the joke rather than turn him into the joke.

But the major smelled fear and couldn't resist. Again he addressed the crowd, which was fast turning into a throng. "Our Captain Ffrench has been commended by the king himself for bravery, my good Londoners. Just the other week he rescued some of these troopers here from the top of a burning building. Yet, as he has just reminded us, he's frightened of heights! Fancy that! Our brave, two-effed Captain F-french f-frightened of heights! Could it be that his previous efforts were performed under the influence of strong drink? Perhaps he is not brave in the least! Perhaps I should send to the king and tell him that his captain F-french is nothing but a f-fraud. What say you, excellent men and women all?"

The major gave Hew a mock shrug. "It's up to y-you, Captain F-f-french," he said. "H-hero or c-coward? Which is it to be?"

Hew looked up. Even the statues of the monarchs in their niches seemed to be taunting him. He could barely see Alice. Sweat prickled his scalp and he was grateful to have at his back the solid shoulder of his horse. Just thinking of heights made him sick. He could not climb up. He could not.

Major Slavering came so close that Hew could see the thickening veins in his eyes. "Can't even do it for a lady?" He leered. "You could do it for the boys," and he began to mince about, pointing at Hew and then at the troopers. The throng howled. The major looked around with intense satisfaction, then began to take off his own coat. "I may only be a poor Slavering, with one s, but I think I can manage to do what is proper by a lady stuck up a monument," he announced, tossing his hat to a delighted small boy to hold. "Get out of my way, Captain Ffrench. I'm going to enjoy myself."

At that moment, from on high, came a small cry. A raven, perched next to Alice on the cornice, was pecking at Uncle Frank's head through the cloak and Alice was kicking at it so hard that she lost her balance. For a second, she rocked backward and forward, her hands paddling crazily, then she dropped clean off the cornice and it was only because, by chance, one hand caught the top of the ledge and the other wedged itself in the egg-and-dart stone patterning that she did not crash all the way down. Had Uncle Frank's head rolled off, Alice would have been lost. However, mercifully, the head remained still. Aghast, Hew ran forward. "Hold on, hold on," he cried. Alice held on.

The major took out a short dagger and put it between his teeth. "She'll put that head back where she got it," he said as he made for the ladder. The dagger nicked the corner of his mouth and a drop of pink saliva glistened, then vanished into the red of his coat. This was too much for Hew. Thrusting aside all his misgivings, he unbuckled his sword, pushed past the major, and began to climb up the ladder himself. He climbed fast, calling out in a voice he hoped was unambiguously good-natured, "I accept your challenge, Major Slavering. I'll get her." Before he could be stopped, or allow his fear to stop him, he was ten feet above the ground and telling himself to remember that he was a captain in Kingston's Light Horse and could do anything he set his mind to.

At first, although high boots hampered him, he made good progress and counted as he climbed, up to ten then back again, up to ten then back again. This helped him to concentrate, but he had no idea at all what would happen when he reached his goal. When he arrived at the top of the ladder he scrambled onto the ledge, then used the scroll to get as near to Alice as he could. He was still too far away to give her his hand, so, unable to think of another plan, he stepped onto the cornice himself and stretched out his arm in the hope that Alice would shuffle up until she reached it.

But Alice had no intention of reaching for anything in a uniform. With her skirt flapping and her heart hammering, she heaved herself back on to the cornice and arranged herself so that she was at least a little less precariously perched. She could hear Hew pleading with her not to be foolish and to come to him, but then she could also hear shouts of "No, no" from down below. The fickle crowd was changing its mind again. Now they did not want Alice to be captured. Those who had been laughing with Major Slavering began to boo and hiss. Slavering hastily remounted his horse. There was no telling how this would end up.

For Alice, there was only one way to go. She must use her fingertips and continue to edge over to the other side of the Bar. If she could make it, she might yet escape. But there were so many obstacles. For a start, the raven, not satisfied with its first attempt, prepared to attack Uncle Frank again, this time with more determination. It was fortunate that, as it swooped down, it spied Uncle Frank's erstwhile neighbor and settled on him, kaw-kawing in its excitement at finding an even easier meal. Alice guessed from the noise what was going on and tried not to be mesmerized by the peck, peck, pecking noises that seemed horribly near her own head. "I will make it, Uncle Frank," she muttered, "I *will* make it." But her resolve was not as certain as she would have liked and when the raven flew past again, ogling her and scattering discolored hailstones of putrefying flesh, Alice found she really could go no farther. Clutching Uncle Frank nearer to protect him, she crouched down and turned to confront the enemy.

Hew, inching along the cornice, was now sweating from every pore. Only iron self-discipline prevented him from throwing himself backward, anything to reach the blessed ground. Sick to his stomach and careless of his dignity, he lay on his side, facing the wall. This was the only way he would be able to move. Time and again, to restore his courage, he reminded himself that if he descended without Alice his life would not be worth living. Already he could hear the crowd beginning a chant of "Coward" and he could just imagine the major's smirking derision. He wiped his cheek on his shoulder, dislodging his hat in the process. He dared not make a grab for it. Moments later he could hear the crowd roar as a sea of eager fingers pulled it apart. He pressed his forehead into the stone.

Hunched like a cornered cat, Alice watched his every move. "Go back," she called out, her voice thin as a bat squeak. "Go back and leave me be."

Hew heard her and gingerly tilted his neck. But the movement was too much for him and he quickly buried it again and the groan he was trying so hard to suppress escaped. Instinctively, Alice put out an arm. But she withdrew it at once. What was she thinking? Hew's groan would be part of a trap. She waited.

"I can't move," Hew said at last. "I am stuck here forever, God help me." His voice was muffled and Alice had to strain for the actual words, but she could hear the shake in them all right and in the face of such weakness she immediately felt better.

"Don't ask God to help you," she retorted, "when I'm hoping he's going to help me."

"I need to get off of here. Please."

"It's a trick." Alice held Uncle Frank's head closer to her. "I'll come near you and you'll grab me."

"No. I swear. I am terrified of heights. I could no more grab you than dance a jig. If you don't help me, I won't get down from here alive."

Alice considered. The sun was fully up and it was getting hot. Her own legs were sore and her head felt too big for her body. She wanted this to be over. "If I help you, will you let me go?" It was the most pathetic of pleas.

Hew strove to be honest. "I wish I could say yes. But I am only a captain. You would have to persuade Major Slavering."

"Is he a man easily persuadable?"

Hew couldn't lie. "Not many people find him so, but you may be different," he said. He shifted slightly and a sliver of masonry disappeared from under his leg. He cried out. His black hair was molded to his scalp.

"What will happen if I do come down with you?" Alice edged slightly nearer, for it seemed to her that the captain really might fall and she did not want that to happen. "Will I be executed?"

"If a jury finds you guilty." Hew could only whisper.

"But I am guilty."

"Perhaps you could put the head back," Hew suggested desperately, his eyes stinging, "then you might just get imprisonment. And I would say that you helped me down from here. That might count in your favor."

"I don't want to be executed. I'm not brave enough." Alice shivered.

"You seem to me to be brave enough for anything," Hew told her, trying to speak in a more normal voice, "and I promise to defend you as best I can."

Alice considered. The one thing she did know was that it was now impossible to desert Hew. How could she, when he was clearly so helpless? She should never have spoken to him. Oh, what was she to do?

A noise from behind helped to make up her mind. On the side of the monument toward which she had been heading, troopers were now waiting. Hew would have to move. "Roll very carefully over onto your stomach and look straight at me," she commanded him. "Just keep looking straight at me and I'll tell you where to go. I'm not good at this myself but I seem to have had quite a lot of practice this morning. Ready?"

Hew fixed his gaze on the small oval face about six feet away and found himself staring straight into a pair of eyes the color of cornflowers. They were wide-set and candid, each iris a pool of such clear, almost icy blue that they would have turned their owner into a cold china doll had not the blurring of the edges by deeper, purple-colored smudges warmed them through. Even in these dire straits, Hew thought them the loveliest things he had ever seen. They regarded him coolly.

"Now," said Alice, not unaware of the effect she had caused, "move from the hip. Right hip just an inch back, then left hip, always in a straight line. Start now. Right hip, left hip, right hip, left hip. I'm going to lie down too, but facing you. We'll be doing it together."

Hew began, repeating her instructions as he went. Their progress was painfully slow, but it was progress. Alice kept Hew's brown eyes entirely in thrall, never letting her own flick away even once. "Left hip, right hip," she said, and hardly realized that by the time they reached the end of the cornice her voice had softened and was almost tender.

When she at last fell silent, they both paused. "You'll have to wriggle until you feel the top of the scroll," Alice told him, noticing the dimple in his chin. His hand was so close, she could have touched it. But she didn't.

Hew pulled himself onto his knees. As he levered himself off, he could still feel cornflower-blue courage pouring through his limbs. Shuffling until his feet found something secure on which to balance, he held out his hand. "Give me the head," he said, "and I'll put it back on the roof."

"Oh no!" Alice's voice was brisker and she was still just out of reach. "I'm not leaving it."

"You must," said Hew.

"I can't."

"I could leave him covered with the cloak." The captain was genuinely sympathetic. "Would you prefer that?"

"No, I wouldn't. His eyes are open," Alice explained. "He wants to be with his body."

"Yes," Hew replied gently, "but it won't help his head if yours is up here too, will it?"

Alice blinked. "I suppose not." She considered, but what Hew suggested was just not possible. "It's my business anyway," she said. "Now go on. Wheesht." It was what her nurse said when Alice was being annoying.

But Hew was not finished yet. "Before we go any further, will you tell me your name?" It was an unusual place for an introduction, but Hew needed to know.

"It's Alice. Alice Towneley."

"I'm Hew. Captain Hew Ffrench."

"I'm not glad to meet you, Captain Ffrench."

Hew blanched. He had hoped for something more friendly than that. "No," he said, recovering, "I don't imagine you are."

"Now get going," ordered Alice, anxious suddenly, and unexpectedly confused. She gripped her cloak harder as she tried to banish Hew's dimple. She must concentrate only on Uncle Frank. She absolutely couldn't leave his head behind. Yet how could she carry it down, when somebody would at once take it from her? She drummed her fingers. She would follow Hew off the cornice, then decide what to do.

In a few minutes she too was on the scroll, then on the wider ledge. Still wary, she insisted that Hew make use of the long ladder before her and looked about, hoping for a miracle. None arrived. Indeed, troopers were now pouring out of the windows. Any second they would have her. With a sinking heart, Alice slithered onto the ladder herself, slinging Uncle Frank onto her back. She would just have to throw herself and Uncle Frank's head on the mercy of Major Slavering. It seemed a vain hope that Captain Ffrench's ability to plead was better than his ability to climb. Nevertheless, it was the only hope Alice had.

She moved slowly, disconcerted by yet another roar from the crowd. She glanced down and found herself looking not at Hew but at Major Slavering himself. He was swinging a padlock and some chains. Even twenty feet up, Alice could see his eyes protruding slightly, for his drinking habits made him bilious, and the expression in them was enough to send her rocketing up the ladder again as quick as she could go. *What a fool I am,* she cried out inside. *I should never have listened to that Captain Hew Ffrench. Oh, how stupid, stupid, stupid!* Yet the top of the ladder held just as many dangers, with troopers waiting in silence. Alice's bottom lip began to tremble.

Slavering, now sure of victory and grinning broadly, turned to shout for a gangway to be made.

He had ordered a cart to transport his prisoner to the jail. Alice heard his shout and screwed up her eyes. She could see the cart. It reminded her of the cart that had taken Uncle Frank to be executed. Indeed, there was even a prisoner kneeling in it with his hands tied behind his back. She shuddered. Then she screwed up her eyes some more and her heart began to beat faster. Goodness! The cart did not just remind her of the one that had taken Uncle Frank. It *was* the one that had taken Uncle Frank. The barrel-chested figure with the cobblestone face and broad shoulders was familiar. Could it be? Oh, if only it was! The man looked up, and Alice knew at once what to do.

When she judged the distance to be about right, she took an enormous breath, pulled Uncle Frank around, and hugged him to her. Then, using one leg, she pushed the ladder away from the wall as hard as she could. "Come on, come on," she prayed. It resisted. Oh, Lord in Heaven! Why was this wretched thing, which had seemed only too keen to keel over before, now trying to behave so responsibly? Alice thumped it as it crashed back against the stones. Then she tried again. It was no good. She could hear the troopers sniggering. On the ground, Major Slavering began to swear. He could see what Alice was trying to do and was determined to prevent her. If she fell off the ladder, she would be dead, and that would be no fun at all. He grabbed a rung, but it was difficult to keep both the ladder and his horse steady simultaneously. He bellowed for help.

Alice went wild. It was now or never. Frantically, she once more rocked the ladder to and fro until the rungs shook. Thud, thud, thud it banged against the wall, thud, thud, thud. It made Alice feel seasick, but though her eyeballs were sliding about, she at last caught sight of Hew. She wanted to shout, but her tongue was stuck, so instead she gestured frantically over his head. Hew frowned for a moment, for it would not do to misunderstand her, then, hardly seeming to move, his face cleared. In an instant, he whipped out his sword and deftly poked the hilt hard into the ribs of Major Slavering's horse. The animal grunted and leaped sideways, knocking the ladder clean for six. Had Alice been able, she would have cheered, but she had no breath, as, with Uncle Frank pressed against her, she was hurled in a great arc through the air. The only noise came from the mob, who screamed as the ladder, in balletic slow motion, crashed into the street and splintered into a thousand scattering pieces.

Alice had abandoned it long before then. At the height of the arc she shut her eyes and let go, while

Dan Skinslicer, his executioner's judgment honed to a T, whipped his horse through the multitude. Although his eyes never left Alice's flying body, he only just caught her, and then at the price of losing his prisoner. As Alice landed, the condemned man was catapulted out of the cart and for the rest of his life made money from relating how he had been saved by an angel of mercy who had flown out of the sky especially for that purpose.

The reality was rather different. The cart sagged as Dan was thrown clean onto his back and the shafts almost broke, crumpling the pony between them. But Dan was quick. Rolling Alice below the seat, he steadied both pony and cart before grabbing his whip and beating anybody who tried to hold on to him. The pony was only too happy to gallop as fast as its stubby legs would carry it down an alley leading away from Temple Bar, even though the alley was so dark and slimy it was like being swallowed by a snake.

Dan could not speak at first, but just hurried the pony along through maze after maze of dingy backstreets until corners and high walls deadened all sounds beyond those they made themselves. When he could no longer make out cries of "Stop, thief!" or "Hang them both!" he began to work his way swiftly past Westminster Bridge, down the bank of the Thames, and into the water meadows beyond. It was some time before he felt it safe to calm the pony's panicky pace, tie the reins in a knot, and bend down to see how his unexpected passenger was faring.

Alice was lying in a small heap, Uncle Frank's head beside her. Dan hardly dared lift up the flap of cloak that hid her face. The girl must be injured. Perhaps she was dead. He hesitated many times before he made himself look, and what he found made him jump. Far from being injured or dead, Alice was smiling a smile as broad as any Dan had ever seen. He was quite taken aback.

She put out her hand. "Oh, Dan Skinslicer," she burst out, "never was I so glad to see anybody as I was to see you, and I know that if Uncle Frank could speak, he would say just the same." She sat up and her smile lost a little of its starriness. "But they'll hang you too now, if they catch you. You can't go home for goodness knows how long. I'm sorry for that."

At first Dan grinned in response, but then he recollected himself and exploded. "What were you doing, missy, up there on the Temple Bar? My heart nearly stopped. Never mind you being pleased to see me, or Colonel Towneley come to that. What would he be saying if he'd seen you flying through the air like one of them circus monkeys? And how'd it be for your mother if next time she clapped eyes on your pretty face it was sitting, without the rest of you, up on the Bar next to the colonel's? And she may yet. Every trooper in the land will be after us by now and we are hardly inconspicuous, you, me, and your uncle Frank's head. We'll be in irons before nightfall and up before Lord Chief Justice Peckersniff by dawn. And to top it all, Lord alone knows who they'll get to hang us. I'll ask if I can do you, but I'm bound to get some clodhopping rope-mangler." He thumped his great fist into the side of the cart, almost knocking a hole through. The pony lurched once again into a trot. Dan picked up the reins. "Happen I'll ask for poison," he said. "There's some say that's an 'angman's privilege. Except old Peckersniff won't go for that," he added gloomily, "not if Major Slavering has anything to do with it. And he will."

Alice looked quite unperturbed. "Oh, we're not going to die," she said, patting Dan's arm reassuringly. "Once or twice today I thought that I might, but now I'm quite sure I'm not, and neither are you. We won't die if we're clever, Dan Skinslicer." She mimicked his gruff accent. "And we are."

Dan looked at his feet. "You may be clever, missy, but not me," he said. "And if they offer me a post in the navy instead of execution, I'll take the execution."

Alice snorted. "You won't have to choose," she declared with a little more confidence than she actually felt. Despite her smile she was still shaking inside, but she didn't want to show Dan. "We'll leave London and go to Towneley. Don't worry, it's miles from the sea. You will be a hero, Dan Skinslicer, especially if you bring home both me and Uncle Frank's head."

"And what exactly will I do at Townswhatever, apart from being a hero?" asked Dan sarcastically. "I don't think you can earn a living standing on a pedestal."

"It's Towneley, and my father will find something," said Alice airily. "He measures rain, you know."

Dan shook his head at her. "What about my wife?" Alice frowned. She had forgotten Johanna. "We could go and get her," she said doubtfully.

Dan's face relaxed a little and eventually he chuckled. "I can just see Johanna in this cart with us: me, her, a papist, and a papist's head. She'd think she'd died and gone to hell. Better leave her be. The mutton pie she made last night wasn't much good in any case. Do you keep a decent kitchen at Tow— Town—whatever?"

"Towneley," repeated Alice patiently, cheery again. "And yes, I think our mutton pies are very tasty, although"—her face darkened a little—"I haven't been home for a bit, so all kinds of things might have changed. They sent me to London to see life, but I seem to have seen more death." She suddenly looked so fragile that Dan wanted to pick her up and put her in his pocket. But scarcely had he thought that than Alice spoke out most robustly. "You'll love my home, Dan Skinslicer, and once we have worked out how to get there, we'll be quite safe. Nobody will ever be bothered to climb over the hills to find us, especially as it's always either foggy or raining. What's more, now that useless Prince Charlie has skedaddled, there's no need for any more rebellions." She decided to give Dan the full benefit of her political opinion. "From now on, Dan Skinslicer, all kings will be called George and people won't care what religion you are."

Alice's tone was highly authoritative and Dan found himself quite happy to believe her. He lost some of his anxious look and wiped his brow as they made their way to the river's edge, mingling easily among the pleasure-seekers. The pony slackened his walk into a meander and began to snatch at tufts of grass. Several times Dan and Alice saw troopers on the road and each tried to reassure the other. But the troopers were idle and none came to accost them. Eventually, in a small hollow, the pony stopped altogether. Alice got out of the cart and unfolded her cloak, glad to see that Uncle Frank had suffered no ill effects. She propped him up, then proudly handed Dan some of the money she had taken from the long case clock. "Take this, Dan Skinslicer," she said. "You may need it for our journey."

Dan did not want to touch the money at first, but Alice insisted, so he carefully counted out several coins, biting each to test its integrity before slipping them into a pouch at his belt. "It's not much, missy," he said, "and we'll need different clothes and a better horse than this if we are to reach Towneley Hall before doomsday."

Alice thought. "We could get clothes from Faraway Granny's house," she said. "Bunion—that's the coachman—is about the same size as you. We could get food too, and a couple of horses. Granny wouldn't mind, although we'd have to avoid Aunt Ursula."

"The dragoons will be watching the house," said Dan. "They will know by now who you are."

"But Granny will be at the wigmaker's tonight," said Alice. "She goes in the closed carriage because she likes to give her bald pate an airing on the way. We could get into the carriage while it is waiting, then sneak through the back door of the house after Bunion has dropped Granny home again. Troopers aren't very bright. They'll watch as Granny gets out at the front, but I'll bet they won't watch when Bunion takes the coach to the coach-house. And don't worry. Granny really won't mind. Actually, she's a bit vague, but I can manage her. Just think, Dan Skinslicer! We'll be right under the troopers' noses and they will never notice. As for creeping out"—Alice wrinkled her own nose very prettily—"well, we'll manage that when the time comes."

Dan looked at her closely. "I believe you are enjoying this," he said with disapproval.

"Bits of it," said Alice, as, quite unsolicited, the image of the black-haired captain's dimple floated into her head. "Bits of it," she repeated a little dreamily, then yelped as she stretched her legs and, quite by mistake, knocked Uncle Frank over.

Dan noted her dreamy look and frowned. Then he began to unhitch the pony. "We won't be needing you anymore, old son," he said a little regretfully, for he was fond of the animal. "Take care of yourself."

Alice gave the pony a pat, then refolded her cloak ready to wrap the head up again, but before she did so she called out, making Dan start. "Look!" Alice was delighted. "Uncle Frank is smiling."

Dan grabbed the cloak and quickly covered the head up. "That's very foolish!" he admonished. "The colonel should wait until we're well on the road north before he goes in for that kind of thing. Now, come on, missy. We've got a wigmaker's to visit." He sighed. "And to think, this time yesterday I was a simple executioner." He should have felt anxious, even aggrieved, but as they set off, and Alice slipped her hand into his, Dan Skinslicer found himself whistling.

4

At dusk, he and Alice made their way in through the poky back door of the wiggery. Nobody stopped them and, when she saw her errant granddaughter, Lady Widdrington simply cocked her head to one side, causing the fussy little wigmaker to trill and flutter as his masterpiece tilted and wobbled.

"What do you think, Alice dear?" Lady Widdrington asked, clamping spiky hands firmly on the purple mountain to avert disaster.

Alice rose at once to the challenge. "It's very striking, Granny, startling even, but in the best possible way."

"I'll make a splash?" The old lady turned back to the mirror.

"I'd say so." Alice took the wrinkled fingers and stroked what skin was visible between the rings. "Granny," she said, keeping her voice low and sweet, "this is my friend Dan Skinslicer."

Dan bowed and as he rose he banged his head on the ceiling. Lady Widdrington turned to stare and

Alice gave him a smile that he did not return. Backing away from the old lady, he knocked a lamp onto the cluttered floor. The burning oil hissed and snippets of horsehair began to sizzle, but when Dan stamped about, trying to put the sparks out, he caused a veritable cascade of wig boxes, wooden models and baskets of samples.

"Oh my very deary me!" exclaimed the wigmaker, cavorting like a fawn as he tried to catch all his goods in his skinny arms. "This is an artisan's shop, not an elephant house! Stay still, large man! Stay still!"

Lady Widdrington scowled but Alice leaped in quickly. "Dan is a friend of Uncle Frank's," she explained, deciding to come if not clean, then cleanish. She would say nothing about Frank being dead. "The thing is, Granny, the dragoons were after Uncle Frank, and Mr. Skinslicer and I helped him escape. I know you will approve of that. But the dragoons are not happy and now we need to escape ourselves." The old lady's watery eyes darted from Alice to Dan and back again. Alice rushed on. "We thought we might just go back to Grosvenor Square with you in the carriage and borrow a few things . . ." She trailed off. Her grandmother's expression was plaintive.

"Where's Frank now?" she asked. "Has he time to see my new wig before you all go gallivantin'?"

Alice relaxed a little. "Not really, Granny dear," she said. "He can't see anything at the moment. But I'll tell him how fine you look. This mauve, it's just the color he'd like."

The wigmaker made approving noises.

Lady Widdrington slid off her chair. "Then I'll take this one, Mr. Wig," she said, for she had clean forgotten the wigmaker's name, though she had used him for thirty years, "and I'll wear it to go, if you don't mind. Give Mr. Skinslicer the wig bag. He can make himself useful carrying it to the carriage."

Mr. Wig rubbed his hands together. "Just the payment, Lady Widdrington," he ventured, hesitating over almost every word. "Even a little of the payment. You have quite a substantial bill here, you know, quite a substantial bill. Could I trouble you for six pounds? My rent is overdue, you see."

Lady Widdrington eyed him with affectionate scorn. "Ah, Mr. Wig," she purred. "You are a splendid craftsman, but, it seems to me, an extremely bad manager of money. You should never owe rent." She wagged her finger. "Instead of paying, I shall do you a favor. I shall keep your money and act as banker. At least then you will always know that you have money safely tucked away in Grosvenor Square." She ignored his look of abject despair. "Come now, Alice. Bunion is waiting and it is rude to take advantage of servants.

Be more careful of your pennies, Mr. Wig—and, Mr. Skinslicer, don't forget the bag."

Dan saw the wigmaker's anguished expression as they negotiated Lady Widdrington's re-entry into her carriage. He looked to see if Alice had noticed, but she was as blithe as if on a picnic. He humphed to himself. Didn't she have a heart? Yet it was impossible not to admire the girl as she skillfully humored her grandmother so that, by the time they got to Grosvenor Square, the old lady was happily conspiratorial, hobbling down the portable steps, her eyes twinkling and one craggy finger on her lips.

The dragoons sent to keep an eye on Lady Widdrington's house had already arrived and, having tied their horses to the railings, were mooching about on foot. They stared with open amusement. What *did* the old witch look like? As Bunion took the carriage away to the stables, they were too busy sniggering to give more than a cursory glance through its dirty windows and Alice and Dan, huddled on the floor, went completely unnoticed.

Alice breathed a sigh of relief. It was all going swimmingly. "What are you doing?" she asked Dan, who was suddenly very busy.

"I'm making the colonel respectable," he told her. "This wig bag will make a fine resting place for him, much better than being bundled up in your cloak. And

I took the liberty of relieving Mr. Wig of some hanks of horsehair as we left, so we can set your uncle Frank up nice and dandy."

"You stole?" Alice was a little shocked.

"I did not." Dan looked hurt. "I left some of your money on a ledge. Which is more than can be said for your grandmother," he added pointedly.

Alice blushed and prickled. "She never takes any money with her. She's frightened of robbers."

"That old woman frightened of robbers! That's rich, young missy, and you can rob without threats and a pistol, you know. Your granny should pay her debts."

There was a frosty silence, then Alice put out her hand. "Don't be cross, Dan Skinslicer," she wheedled.

Dan shook her away. "I'm not cross," he said stubbornly. "I'm just pointing out the truth. Your granny is as much of a thief as a pickpocket."

Alice set her lips and tossed her head. "That's a very rude thing to say."

"I don't care." Dan refused to give in. "Mr. Wig has to earn his money and if your granny doesn't give it to him, that means she has robbed him. Simple as that." He didn't need a lamp to feel Alice smarting in the dark. They did not speak again until the yard gates swung shut behind them.

Alice peered cautiously out of the window. "I was right," she said, and did not try to conceal the triumph in her voice. "There are no dragoons around here. Lazy creatures."

"They do their job," said Dan, still unforgiving. "Do you know, sometimes they're given oatmeal instead of silver as their pay?" He peered out of the window too. "And some of them don't even like oatmeal," he hissed very close to Alice's ear.

She opened her mouth, then thought the better of it. Anyway, there was no time, for as soon as Bunion climbed off the box they had to take their chance. Slipping out of the carriage as lightly as they could, they skittered across the yard with Uncle Frank's head swinging in its bag, then in through the back door of the house, taking refuge in alcoves and storerooms until they were clear of the servants' quarters and in the main hall. From here, Alice had hoped to spirit Dan directly up the stairs to her room.

But unfortunately Lady Widdrington was waiting. Thoroughly excited by both Alice and Dan's appearance at the wiggery and her new, magnificent hairpiece, she was calling for supper and minstrels. "Alice!" she cried, "Alice, and your friend, whose name I forget! Go around the square and gather everyone up. While you are doing that, I shall find out if there is an officer or two among those men in handsome uniforms who are hanging around the railings. Maybe a major, or even a general? Perhaps they have already heard of my new wig and that's why they are here." She began to hop over to the door, but found the back of her skirts trodden on hard.

"No, Granny, no!" Alice's voice was a squeal.

The old lady started to dislike her granddaughter's tone. "Alice dear," she said icily, "this is my house and I shall do what I like. Ursula! Ursula!"

There was a pause. Alice and Lady Widdrington glared at each other until Ursula clacked down the stairs, her own wig awry and her expression dazed. She had been tucked up in bed asleep. When she saw Alice, she opened her mouth to scold, but when she saw Dan, she gulped, for although his clothes were scruffy, his air of rough gentility was, to Ursula, quite irresistible. "Oh!" she said, smoothing her nightgown. "Hello!" And she sidled across the room.

"Ursula!" Lady Widdrington squawked her disapproval. "This man is not for you. He's, er, he's a, oh dear, he's something—" Alice tried to help, but her grandmother ignored her. Then her face lit up. "He's the children's new dancing master. Isn't that right, Alice?"

Alice edged Dan nearer to the stairs and nodded. "That's right, Granny," she agreed, not meeting Ursula's eye. Her hair stood on end when she thought of what her aunt would do if she knew the truth or guessed what was in the wig bag. "He's our dancing master."

Lady Widdrington grew quite gay. "And we are to have a gavotte before bed," she cried. "I once danced the gavotte at court in France." She touched her sinewy throat, remembering the diamonds that had sparkled there when it was smooth and white. "My partner, a count no less, told me I was exquisite, exquisite." She began to tap back and forth, her small feet like a pair of antique beetles. "Do you hear that, Ursula? Has any man ever thought you exquisite? Perhaps a blind man?" She held her arms out to Dan. "Now, come, man, come."

Dan stood his ground. "I can't dance and I'll not be made an idiot," he muttered to Alice. "Let's collect what we came for and get out of this madhouse." He turned and put one boot on the stairs.

"She's not mad, she's just forgetful," Alice muttered back, trying to smile at her grandmother, who was clearly displeased at Dan's reluctance. "She's not trying to make a fool of you, Dan Skinslicer, but I'm afraid— oh dear." Alice held her breath.

Lady Widdrington had forgotten her gavotte. She was, instead, gazing beadily at the wig bag now tucked under Dan's arm and, before Alice could blink, had darted across the room and grabbed at it. There was a brief struggle, with the result that the bag went bowling across the floor, leaving Dan with only a tassel. Quick as a flash, he set off in pursuit, Lady Widdrington skipping in front of him. She reached the bag first and Dan did the only thing he could think of: he picked the old lady up bodily and parked her, like a rag doll, on the table. Then he snatched Uncle Frank back and, with Alice right behind him, belted up the stairs.

Immediately the old lady set up a mewling, thrumming her heels on the tabletop. "The man's a thief! He's stolen my new hair! Stop him! Stop him!" In her confusion, she had quite forgotten that her new wig was not actually in the wig bag but safely on her own head. "Send for Bunion. Send for Frank! Catch him!"

Ursula, who had been standing, slack-jawed, was now galvanized into action. Running to the front door, she threw it open and appeared, a skeletal apparition in yards and yards of crumpled lace. "We have a thief," she cried theatrically. "Come, men, come and save us." The dragoons stared, incredulous.

A voice came from behind. "Gather your weapons, men!" It was Hew Ffrench, sent to oversee the night watch. "You heard the lady." And with six troopers behind him, he ran inside.

"Up the stairs," Ursula commanded, stretching out an arm and throwing back her head in a posture she associated with goddesses, "he's run up the stairs."

Hew set off and the troopers clanked faithfully after him.

Alice heard the jingle of swords and was in agony. "Hurry, hurry!" she urged Dan as they fled along the passages, blowing out the lamps as they went. There was no time to find a decent hiding place and the dark was their only hope. "We'll go to my bedroom," Alice panted at last. "I've a huge wardrobe. It's worth a try, and anyway, I can't think of anywhere else. Hurry, Dan Skinslicer, hurry."

She pushed Dan through an open door, locked it as quietly as she could, and bundled him into the wardrobe among all her dresses. Clutching the wardrobe key, she dived under her bed. It was a silly hiding place, she knew that, but the door was already being tried and Captain Ffrench was already shouting that the thief had better open it or he would batter it down. Noises of battering followed soon after. Alice lay there, trying to quiet her breathing. The floor was foul and she could feel it alive with creeping things. One began to crawl up her nose but she didn't dare move to brush it away. Against her cheeks, soft balls of fluff drifted and sticky dust soon coated her lips. She tried not to breathe, but it was no good. The dust followed the creepy-crawly up her nose and, just as her bedroom door splintered, she sneezed. It was such a powerful sneeze that her head jerked upward and hit hard on the wooden mattress slats. Only a person made of stone could have avoided yelping and Alice was not made of stone.

In a minute, Hew Ffrench was on his knees, dragging her out and shining a candle in her face. When he saw that, far from a thief, it was Alice, he was completely disconcerted. "You!" he exclaimed. Then he was angry. Why on earth had Alice come back here? She must have known that it was the most dangerous place in town. He had imagined her well away by now. He turned to his men, whose swords were drawn and raised. "Sheathe your weapons," he ordered. "This lady's not a thief."

"She is," said one of the dragoons insolently, peering down and instantly recognizing Alice, despite her dirty face. "As you well know, Captain Ffrench, she's the reason we 'ave to stand out there in the street instead of enjoying ourselves in the tavern." He turned to his fellow troopers. "Here's that wench as stole that traitor's 'ead from Temple Bar. She must 'ave crawled in 'ere when we wasn't lookin'."

His fellow troopers hooted with excitement and were all for marching Alice instantly away. But then Aunt Ursula appeared in the doorway, tutting with annoyance. "That's not the thief, that's Alice," she announced, exasperated. "The thief was a man. A big person, much bigger than Alice." She had visions of

Dan being taken and then saved from hanging by her eloquence. He'd have to marry her then. But first he had to be found.

"No," Alice insisted to Hew. "There was nobody else. Aunt Ursula just wants you to think that because she doesn't want you to take me away. There really was nobody else. Just think about it. No man would risk being hung as a thief for something as silly as a wig."

Ursula was affronted. "There was a man," she said, "a fine-looking man, and I think it very selfish, Alice, to keep him to yourself."

Alice stamped her foot. "There was no man, Aunt. Or only in your dreams. Go back to bed."

"What nonsense." Ursula grew more and more dogged. She now eyed Captain Ffrench from handsome top to handsome toe. "He was a strapping man built of logs," she said, touching her lips to see if there was any rouge still on them. "That's what he was. He must be in here somewhere. Please catch him, or I shall be too afraid to do anything except stand quaking in my nightgown." She gave a girlish smile and showed off surprisingly trim ankles. But Hew never saw them for he was trying to stop Alice from attacking two troopers who were heading for her wardrobe. Quietly but deftly, he pinned her arms to her sides. When the troopers carelessly wrenched off the wardrobe doors, she was beside herself. "It's very rude, Captain

Ffrench," she shouted, writhing as hard as she could, "to search among a lady's clothing. It's really very rude."

Hew regarded her as she defied him. He was not thinking of her wardrobe. "Now we have found you, we must arrest you," he said sorrowfully. "You are guilty of stealing a traitor's head. Do you understand what the penalty is for that?"

Alice would not let her eyes drop, but she found that her voice had become quite small. "Yes." She shivered pitifully, then turned the shiver into a more matter-of-fact shake. "Leave this silly search and just arrest me now. I'll come with you. There is nothing here. Let's get it over with."

Hew nodded and gestured to the men, but one, a hefty fellow with a sly expression, did not at once obey. "I'll just run my sword through these dresses, Captain, to make sure there really are no other criminals being harbored here," he said, with a false and unpleasant grin. "I'll do it with my eyes shut to save your blushes, mistress, and apologies in advance for the rips." He winked ostentatiously at Hew and, before Alice could say a word, he had his companions roaring with mirth as he thrust and parried in a pretend duel with a rustling mass of silks and bows. He saved his last flourish for a Prussian-blue velvet evening gown of which Alice was particularly proud. The velvet was thick and defended itself well, but when the trooper had finished, it would not even have made a decent duster.

Not that Alice cared. Hew watched very carefully as all the color left her face and her legs turned to jelly. He glanced over at the wardrobe, then made a decision. "We'll leave you to get yourself ready for prison," he told her. "You may like to change into warmer clothes, for the cells are cold and damp. In five minutes, I will come up and take you away. Five minutes," he repeated pointedly.

Alice nodded mutely but Ursula, standing with her hands splayed over her cheeks as if to prevent her head from taking off, was loud in her consternation. "Prison? Damp? Oh no! The child will catch her death and then I'll somehow be to blame. It's too bad. Alice, I really think—" But Alice never learned what her aunt thought, for Hew took a firm hold of Ursula's bony elbow, hustled her out, and shut what remained of the door.

As soon as their footsteps faded, Alice grabbed a candle, flew to the wardrobe, and tore down the clothes. Dan was slumped on the floor. "Dan Skinslicer! Dan! Oh, Dan!" She tried to pull him into her arms, but he was too heavy. As she tugged, he groaned and opened his eyes. Alice rocked back on her heels. "At least you're alive," she wept. "Oh Lord! That terrible sword. It is all my fault. I'm so sorry!"

Dan lay there, a red stain spreading pointed fingers down his shirt. The sword had sliced into his shoulder, causing a gaping flesh wound. Once he realized that by great good fortune he was not dying, however, and that the injury, though unsightly, was relatively light, he began to enjoy Alice's tearful remorse, so took his time before rolling out of the wardrobe and into a sitting position. Alice set down the light and began tearing strips from her ruined dresses, bringing bowls of water from her ewer. She cleaned the wound, packed it with wadding, and bound it up. Dan followed her every movement, liking the cool, expert touch of her hands, and when she had finished, he had to make quite an effort to give a grimace of pain.

Alice narrowed her eyes, then jumped up, flushing rosily. "Now then, Dan Skinslicer." She wrung out the cloths. "Let's not waste any more time. You heard Captain Ffrench. They're going to arrest me any minute now and God alone knows what they will do if they catch you. There's only one way to go." She ran to the door to see if she could block it up to give them a little longer, but it was too badly broken. She ran back to Dan. "If you feel up to it," she said, "we must get out of the window." She hesitated. "Or perhaps you should go alone, taking Uncle Frank of course, and I should give myself up." She crumpled a little. "Or perhaps we should just leave Uncle Frank here. Help me, Dan Skinslicer. I don't know what to do."

Dan pulled his shirt back over his shoulder. "We may disagree about thieving and paying people," he said at once, "but I'm not leaving you to be taken to Major Slavering, that I'm not. We'll try the window."

"And Uncle Frank?"

"We'll take him with us. If we don't and they find him, your grandmother and aunt'll be for the chop. We can't let that happen, can we?"

There was only a moment's pause. "Of course not," said Alice. It was an effort to sound absolutely firm. Dan frowned at her, but let it pass. "Right then, we'd best be going." He got up, winced, and with one heave threw open the heavy sash. "These newfangled things really do work," he said. "Now, come on."

Alice took a deep breath as she looked down. The darkness blurred the height but she could hear the dog whining in the yard far below. Using Dan's strong arms for reassurance, she slid out and, using his hands as a stepping stone, pulled herself up into the guttering. From there she could lean down, shaky but not insecure, to take Uncle Frank's wig bag. Dan came hastily after her, ignoring the stabs of complaint from his shoulder. It was not easy, but the thought of Major Slavering and the dragoons was enough to give him extra spring.

Carefully, they began to make their way across the sloping slates, feeling every inch. Several times Alice slipped and was saved from falling only by the solid mass of Dan behind her. He grunted slightly as her heels dug into him but did not give way. Alice was filled with gratitude. Never had she met anybody so dependable.

Even before they reached the lead part of the roof, which was easier and flatter, they could hear the commotion caused by the discovery of both Dan's bloodied rags and their escape. Shouts and roars spilled out and lamps were waved around. Hew's voice was very clear as he stuck his head briefly through the window sash. Alice and Dan froze. If Hew chose to swing his light upward, he would surely see them. But Hew steadfastly looked the other way. "They're both gone," he called to his men. "Outside, quick. We may find them yet." And with that he vanished. Alice leaned against a chimney pot, almost tearful with relief. Then Dan was pushing her on.

They climbed the whole way along one side of Grosvenor Square before stopping, too tired to struggle further when they seemed, for the moment at least, secure enough. It was a warm night and the sky was dotted with stars. As they flopped down, Alice squeezed Dan's good arm. "He let us go, that Captain Ffrench," she said.

Dan resented the admiration in Alice's tone. "His men damn nearly killed me," he reminded her. "My shoulder's still bleeding. It's going to be a dratted nuisance until it heals and we aren't clear yet, missy, not by a long way."

"Are you in a lot of pain?" Alice was full of commiseration and Dan's heart softened.

"I dare say I've hurt some of my clients more." He sounded much more conciliatory as he opened his shirt so that she could have another look. Alice unwrapped the wound, inspected it, then dextrously bound it up again. "Who taught you that?" Dan asked, admiring.

"My nurse," said Alice. "She taught me almost everything I know."

"I'm sure your mother wouldn't like to hear you say that."

"Oh, she wouldn't mind," said Alice with a happy smile. "She spends most of her life saying the rosary. She really wanted to be a nun, only inheritance and all that meant she had to marry somebody. All her brothers died, you see, and her sister, Ursula—well, you've seen Ursula. Who'd marry her? Mother was lucky, really, ending up with Father. He spends so much time measuring rain that she can pray all she wants. She makes cheese too. It's a very fine arrangement."

Dan listened as Alice wittered on. They made themselves comfortable. Only when the chatter stopped did he begin to think, a little guiltily, about his own wife, now abandoned and penniless. Johanna was a nag and a millstone, but she was his wife. He owed her something. But then he felt Alice's fingers, light and dainty on his brow, testing his temperature in case his wound brought fever with it. "I can't go home yet," he said to himself quite reasonably. "Everybody will know by now that it was me who got missy here and Colonel Towneley away from Temple Bar. We're in this together. When I've got Mistress Alice safely to Towneley Hall, then I'll send for Johanna." And with that he put his conscience uneasily but thankfully to bed.

5

He must have dropped off for a few moments because he was woken by Alice digging him in the ribs. It was still dark, but Alice no longer felt safe. From below, the shouting of the troopers was increasing in volume. Dragoons were stationed all over now, in the knowledge that their quarry must at some stage descend. Alice knew that Hew could hardly order them to leave without putting himself under fire for neglecting his duty. "If we are going to get home, Dan Skinslicer," Alice was thinking aloud, "we'll have to get into somebody else's house and see if we can get out from there."

Dan's shoulder was throbbing but he responded to Alice's prodding as best he could. Cautiously, they made their way to the parapet and peered over. It was impossible, from this angle, to see if any windows were open, so Alice, raising her eyebrows, pulled off the two underskirts she was wearing, then ripped and twisted them into the longest rope they could make.

She tied one end around her own waist and the other end around Dan's. Now she could lean over a little farther.

The nearest windows were tightly closed, but one a little way along was open at the top, with heavy curtains drawn over it. She tugged the rope and, when Dan pulled her back toward him, whispered that this was the one.

The plan seemed full of danger to them both, and by Alice's calculations they also needed more rope, so to Dan's acute embarrassment, since the petticoat rope was almost too much for him, Alice hitched up her skirts again and took off both her stockings. Using one to attach the wig bag to her belt, she gave the other to Dan to wedge anywhere he could find to help him climb down after her. *Thank goodness Johanna can't see me now*, Dan thought.

Even though firmly attached to Dan's immovable middle, it was perilous easing onto the window ledge, particularly with Uncle Frank swinging beside her, and Alice's fingers scrabbled against the wall as she bumped her knees. It seemed ages before she found the comforting solidity of the ledge. The wig bag bruised her hip as she steadied herself, but Alice made no sound. Carefully, she put two hands on the sash and leaned her weight against it. It slid down so smoothly that she momentarily lost her balance and her feet swung up behind her. Then she righted herself and slithered over, dragging Uncle Frank behind her. She could not get farther into the room because the petticoat rope was not long enough, but through the divide in the curtains she could see that she was in a bedroom. What was more, the snores that were causing the oak four-poster to quiver were louder than any noise two fugitives were likely to make breaking in. Luckier still, the bed's occupants, clearly nervous of drafts, were cocooned behind thick hangings garishly embroidered with naked cherubs.

She turned to see how Dan was getting on. After a moment or two, she heard his toes scuff the window ledge. Alice grasped an ankle and guided it toward the sill. Dan was grunting terribly and Alice longed to tell him to be quiet, but before she could put her fingers to her lips she herself cried out as she was almost whisked back through the window. Dan's other foot missed the sill and, with a terrible "Oio! Oio!," he began to topple backward. At once Alice found herself jerked upward by the petticoat rope. Clinging to the curtains until they threatened to come down on top of her, she just managed to spread-eagle herself against the window frame, praying that this would give Dan enough leverage to pull himself back. Every sinew objected as she stretched out, muscles pulled beyond endurance, to provide a bulwark for Dan's body, which was now swaying like a bag of flour. She could hear him swearing, but what good was that? The pressure around her middle grew intolerable. She was going to be squeezed in half! Tighter and tighter grew the rope until Alice saw only red. Surely her waist could get no smaller? But it did. Then, just as her legs dissolved into mush, the pressure relaxed and she found Dan on the other side of the glass, his mouth open and his eyes wide. He trembled like a great tree in autumn as he fumbled his way clumsily over the window frame and into the bedroom. It was not a noiseless maneuver, but Alice no longer cared. When he finally galumphed onto the floor, she threw her arms around his neck as though she would never let him go. The couple in the bed snored on.

When they managed to regain some composure, Dan undid the petticoat rope and hid it under a large commode. Then he took the wig bag from Alice because her arms felt too weak to carry it and they crept together across the room. A floorboard creaked and Dan and Alice crouched down as oaths were muttered in a deep, throaty voice, followed by higher-pitched womanish grumbles. Somebody belched but nothing more. When the snoring was firmly re-established, Alice scrutinized the monograms embroidered on the clothes draped untidily over an overflowing laundry basket. She began tugging them out, pointing excitedly. Dan looked unconvinced but Alice nodded her head vigorously and soon both they and Uncle Frank were buried deep inside the basket under mounds of aristocratic dirty linen.

"I know the people in the bed—or at least one of them," Alice whispered, her lips against Dan's cheek. "This is the Duke of Mimsdale's house. I don't know who is in bed with him but it's certainly not his wife. She's away. So I bet the maids will come in the morning and load anything that might tell a naughty tale onto a cart for the laundryman. If we're lucky, this basket will be transported miles away from here. We might even be able to jump out as it goes on its way."

"And what happens if the duchess isn't due back for weeks and the housekeeper decides the laundry can wait?" Dan hissed back. Alice never seemed to think of these things. "I don't think I can stay scrunched up in here for days, with all these unsavory undergarments and sweaty sheets, even if they do belong to a duke."

"Well," Alice said, taking the wig bag and making a nest for it as she settled herself against Dan's shoulder, "I think it is our best chance."

Dan could not dispute this and after a while, in the peaceful warmth of ruffles and petticoats, both of them fell into a much deeper sleep than either would have thought possible under the circumstances.

A good jolting woke them. It was broad daylight and the laundry basket was being pushed across the floor by two female servants, amazed at its weight.

"What's the duke put in here?" one asked the other, "'er Grace's body?"

The other, between pants, bade her friend be silent. "Never joke about that sort of thing in this house," she snorted. "Old Mimsy hates his duchess. She may well be in here for all I know, but it won't do us any good to find her."

There was no more chat as the basket thudded down the stairs and sailed across the marble floor toward the front door, where it took four footmen to load it onto the flat wagon waiting to receive it.

Hew's troopers, scattered all over the square, were immediately suspicious. "Open it," one ordered the laundryman.

"What for?"

"Just do as I say. We're looking for two criminals who escaped around here and they might be inside."

The laundryman shrugged and beckoned to the footmen. "Open it for the king's dragoons," he said. "They want to see if the duke has criminals in his washing."

The footmen were reluctant, but the troopers were persistent. One, with youthful arrogance, flicked his sword lazily against the wicker. "Do you want me to open it?" he asked.

The nearest footman looked nervous. If there was damage to the duke's property, he would be made to pay. He began to fumble and had almost got the strap undone when a cough made him look up.

"Er, excuse me. What do you think you're doing?" The Duke of Mimsdale, chewing a fat chicken leg, was watching from an upper window. As a rule he cared little for his laundry, but, with his wife in the country, he did not want his sheets displayed to the entire square. "Take the laundry away," he ordered, waving his hand.

But the troopers were not frightened of old Mimsy. Everybody knew that he had fallen out with the king, and those out of favor with the king were not due any respect. A veteran trooper stood his ground. "Go and get Major Slavering," he ordered his young colleague. "We'll see about this."

Inside the basket, Alice and Dan lay quaking.

Some curious onlookers gathered and when the major, accompanied by Hew, pushed through on horseback, an expectant hush fell. The duke, with his boots on but still not properly dressed, appeared on the doorstep and strode out, hoping to cow everybody with both the size of his paunch and the acres of gold frogging on his red silken dressing gown. Major Slavering and Hew dismounted and handed their horses to the cornet.

"Good day to you," the duke began, in his grandest voice. "Is there some trouble with my laundry?"

The major eyed him up and down, noting the nervous tic in the ducal eyelid. "Two criminals, plus a head, are loose in the square. They may be so desperate to escape, Your Grace"—he accentuated the title, making it ridiculous—"that they might even brave your dirty washing. They have slipped through the clutches of Captain Two-Effs Ffrench twice now. This is his last chance."

The duke flapped the ends of his wig, feeling a little hot. "I can assure you, Major," he said, "that, as a loyal subject of King George, I would not conceal enemies of His Majesty in my laundry. My laundry is an entirely private affair, not open to criminals or anybody else. I'm sure, being a man of the world yourself"—he bared his teeth queasily at the major— "you understand that I would like to keep it that way."

"It's a big laundry basket for a small duke, though." Major Slavering enjoyed making Mimsy sweat. With a gloved finger, he traced the coronet engraved on the leather strap. "A very big basket indeed. So big"— he trailed his fingers all the way along its length— "that I'm truly impressed. You must be the cleanest man in England and it would be a fine thing for my men to see that clothes and sheets do not have to be crawling with lice before they meet soap and water. Come, sir. Open the basket. Even if we find no criminals, we'll find something to interest us, I dare say."

The duke could see the game was up. With a fixed smile, he ordered his footmen to undo the strap and throw back the lid.

There was nothing Dan and Alice could do. They held hands as the top sheets were hauled out and spread on the pavement, along with shirts and other garments that made the duke mutter, "Really, really." Little by little the basket was emptied, until discovery was imminent. The spectators were laughing uproariously as Alice, who could just about squint through the weave, poked Dan and whispered in his ear. The next sheet slid away from them. Alice's throat was too dry to shout, but Dan just heard her croak "Now!" before, with nothing left to lose, they sprang up together, extraordinary figures draped in cambric and gauze, with fine woolen bloomers wound about their heads.

Vaulting over the side of the basket, they startled the cornet into dropping the reins of the horses belonging to Hew and Major Slavering, and Alice, gesticulating wildly, clutched a stirrup, and threw herself over one of the saddles. Dan, less elegantly, followed suit. Terrified, the horses took fright and galloped away as fast as they could, with Dan and Alice hanging on for dear life. The crowd scattered before them, and the laundry horse, which had not been out of a walk for a decade, also took to his heels and set off at a spanking trot. Around Grosvenor Square they all pelted, Dan and Alice in front and the lumbering laundry horse behind, spreading stockings and pillowcases like giant confetti. One large, bright-red nightgown, clearly not the property of a duchess, ballooned into the sky before settling gracefully around the shoulders of Major Slavering himself. Livid, he fought it off, but the sleeves clung about his neck and even the troopers could hardly contain their giggles. Whirling like a tornado, the major eventually managed to disentangle himself, but not before being assailed by a woman's camisole and a nightcap clearly marked "Mimikins." Now Major Slavering's blood was really up. He, who had braved the muskets and broadswords of the Scottish rebels without blanching, would not be humiliated by some trumpery hat. He ground his teeth and swore horrible vengeance. Hew would pay for this; by all God's saints, he would pay.

Lady Widdrington, hearing the rumpus, ordered Ursula to throw open their windows. She was fond of riots and this sounded like a good one. As Alice and Dan galloped by a second time, the old lady recognized them and waved. "That's my girl," she cried, imagining that she was at the racecourse. "Did we have a gamble, Ursula?"

But Ursula hardly heard her. "Alice is riding astride, and she's NO STOCKINGS ON!" she shrieked. "The shame! The shame! What will my poor sister say when she hears of this?"

"Oh, pishy wishy, Ursula. Don't be such a stick," scolded her mother. "This is better than being at war!" She pinched her daughter's cheek and leaned farther out of the window. Now she forgot about the race-course and saw Alice as a tragic heroine. "Fly, fly to your uncle Frank, Alice my lovely!" she sang out, as if at the theater, and waved her hands, then, feeling this was not enough for such an occasion, she took off her wig and waved that too. "Fly to your uncle Frank!" Purple dust liberally sprinkled the heads and shoulders of those below.

Alice could see her grandmother clearly, but only caught the last echo of her words. Despite the heat of the chase, they made her go cold all over. Uncle Frank's head! She had left it behind! She glanced over her shoulder. The laundryman had caught his horse and the major was now mounted on another. Hew had charge of the washing basket.

Alice turned. "Dan!" she shouted into the wind, "Dan, we've forgotten Uncle Frank!" But Dan could do nothing except twist his hands deeper into his horse's mane. He had never ridden before and was quite out of control, and anyway there was no going back. Even

Alice must know that. They would have to leave Uncle Frank where he was. Alice punched herself with fury. How could she have been so thick? Without Uncle Frank's head, the point of all this was totally lost.

However, even she had to accept that it would not help Uncle Frank if she and Dan were taken too. Glancing around, she saw with some relief that the spectators, clearly wanting the funfair spectacle to last as long as possible, had closed ranks behind her, keeping the major and the pursuing troopers momentarily at bay. Taking full advantage, Alice pushed her horse as close as she could to Dan's, seized its flapping rein, and steered both animals helter-skelter up to the main road. Here, all the assorted traffic of a London morning was building up: coaches, wagons, donkeys, children walking in pairs to school. Alice and Dan plunged through the lot, but though people shouted, most were too intent on their own business to pay much attention to a stockingless girl and an ashen-faced man, even if they were going at a pace more commonly seen at Newmarket. People were always fleeing from something or other. Best not to get involved.

Alice kept charge of both horses as well as she could, trying neither to lose Dan nor to knock anybody over. "Passage, passage!" she cried. "Please let us through!"

The crowd grumbled but obliged, and by the time the major managed to get away from Grosvenor

Square, she and Dan were heading northward through emptier streets and lanes until they eventually found themselves in the fields beyond Marylebone. The horses' blood was up and, as the country spread wide in front of them, Hew's black took the bit between his teeth. The feel of the girl's bare legs was strange to him, as was her gossamer touch on the bit in his mouth. In the end, Alice had to let go of Dan's horse, although she could still hear Dan's groans as his bottom was battered against the army saddle.

Alice steered right away from the main road and into the fields, plunging in and out of woods until, certain that they had outrun their pursuers, she hauled on the reins, aimed the horse into a thicket, and finally managed to bring him to a halt. She leaped off at once and in a second Dan was beside her. He did not leap off, but simply let go and fell to the ground in a style that left his horse distinctly unimpressed.

Alice slumped down next to him, tears streaming down her face. "Uncle Frank," was all she could say. "How could I have left him behind, Dan Skinslicer? How could I? He'll be back on Temple Bar before we know it and I'll have to start all over again."

It was a while before Dan could answer, but when he did, he was quite emphatic. "You most certainly will not, missy," he stated, grimacing as he sat up, for the whole of him was in agony. "Are you mad? We're going nowhere near Temple Bar."

"But we can't leave Uncle Frank to Major Slavering. Just imagine what he will do."

"Well, we'll have to leave your uncle Frank to get on as best he can for the time being. Gracious! We only just escaped with our heads ourselves. Are you never content?" Dan's temper was short, not only because of his lively aches and pains, but also because he was starving, having had nothing to eat since before going to the wiggery. He didn't care if Alice looked mutinous. "I never thought that the laundry basket was a good idea," he added reasonably, although not very kindly.

"Did you have a better one?"

"Well, no," he admitted. "But maybe I would have thought of one in time."

"But we didn't have any time, Dan Skinslicer. That's the point." Alice's voice was deliberately stinging.

The horses began to graze and Dan got up. "It's no good blaming each other," he said. "Let's look on the bright side. We've lost your uncle, but we've two fine horses. What we need now is a good breakfast, some different clothes, and a new plan." He nudged Alice gently, not wanting to see her cross. They were stuck with each other for the time being. "And you never know. Maybe it'll be that Captain Ffrench who gets charge of Uncle Frank and not Major Slavering," he said, and this was generous of him, for the thought of Hew was still irksome. "If he puts the colonel's head back on the Bar, at least he'll do it nicely."

Dan's face was so honest and sensible, and he was trying so hard, Alice was ashamed of herself. She gave him a gentle hug. "You're right, Dan Skinslicer," she said, "and what's more, you are a good man to have in moments of trouble—even if you can't ride."

"I can learn," said Dan stoutly, returning Alice's hug with an awkwardness that had nothing to do with his injured shoulder. He extricated himself and eyed the major's horse balefully. "At least, I suppose I could learn. I'm really better with ponies and carts. These horses are too grand for me and this one knows it."

Alice laughed. "I'll make a horseman out of you before we get to Towneley," she promised, swishing her bare legs through the reeds. "Now. Clothes, food—and Uncle Frank's head. Which will you take charge of?"

Dan sighed. Alice was not going to give up. "All of them," he said, "but I'll walk back into town on my own. There's lots of folk about so nobody will notice a scruffy man on foot and I know my way around better than you. I'll see what I can pick up."

"Do you have enough money?"

Dan felt in his pouch. "I have none," he said sorrowfully. "It must have all emptied itself in that dratted basket."

"I have lost mine too," said Alice. She opened her eyes, all innocence. "So how will somebody who disapproves of stealing get what we need?" She couldn't resist teasing.

"I'll do it my own way," said Dan, turning rather grumpy, "and anyway, this is different. This is an emergency."

"At least we can agree about that." Alice took one large hand between both of hers to rub his temper away, then she got up. "I want to come with you, but I suppose somebody has to keep the horses. Be back by evening, Dan Skinslicer. If you're not, I shall come looking for you."

Quick as a flash, Dan was in front of her, seizing her and looking her square in the face. "If I'm not back by evening," he said, deadly serious, "Uncle Frank's head or no Uncle Frank's head, you get on that horse and ride as fast and hard as you can over those hills until you get home. You hear me? You ride straight home. I'll not go unless you promise me, on the dead colonel's soul, to do that."

Alice tried to wriggle away but Dan easily held her. "You promise me," he said, and shook her hard. "On the dead colonel's soul, promise."

"All right, I promise," said Alice reluctantly. "I promise, on Uncle Frank's soul."

Dan made her repeat this and only then, with many

misgivings, did he let go. There was nothing he wanted to do less than trudge down the road up which he had galloped so uncomfortably only moments before. There was nothing in the world he wanted to do less than leave Alice. But there was no option. He turned around just once before he was out of sight and opened his mouth to call to her. But Alice was not looking his way: she was fully occupied petting Hew's horse. Dan shook his head, cursing himself for being nothing but a soppy mooncalf. Then he shut his mouth and, with weary resignation, headed back toward danger.

Stranded with the laundry basket, Major Slavering's parting glare still hot on his face, Hew also felt foolish. He was too polite to curse Alice, but he did wish that she had found a less lively way of leaving Grosvenor Square and that she had not taken his horse. He could get another horse, of course, but he had been fond of Marron, who had cost him a pretty penny. Slavering's horse, Belter, had been expensive too, and looking at the major's face as he fought his way up the road on a rather lowly, borrowed beast, Hew knew that if Dan and Alice were ever caught, their list of offenses would be long and grim. Treachery, thieving, resisting arrest, and now horse stealing. Hew paled at the punishments. On his left, the Duke of Mimsdale was grumbling away as his linen and clothes were collected and given to maidservants to fold. Hew itched to tell the silly old fool to shut up, but he did not. Instead, to hasten the process, he helped repack the basket.

It was while shoving half a dozen petticoats down the side that he felt the wig bag. It was a strange thing to find in a laundry basket and it brought him up short. When Alice and Dan had leaped out, he had hardly expected them to be swinging Uncle Frank's head by its hair. In fact, he had not really been thinking about the head at all. But now that he was thinking about it, everything fell into place. Of course! What better place to hide a head than a wig bag? He looked cautiously around.

The major, grim-faced, had returned empty-handed from pursuing Alice and Dan, his temper beyond filthy. Troopers from all over the city would be dispatched to search out the fugitives like animals, for the major would not be made an idiot of anymore. Hew knew Slavering in this mood. To hand over Uncle Frank's head now would not pacify him or make him less likely to pursue Alice to the death. Rather the opposite. He would pursue Alice using the head as some disgusting form of blackmail, probably to lure her into a trap from which there would be no escape. Hew frowned. He must extricate the wig bag before the laundryman found it but without Slavering seeing. He began, cautiously, to pull at it, then stopped. What on earth was he doing? Why was he risking not only his own life but the lives of his mother and sister, his only remaining family, for a girl he hardly knew?

It was a silly question because he already knew the answer. The memory of Alice's cornflower eyes and the radiating confidence with which she had saved him at Temple Bar floated constantly about his head, knocked into his heart, and disturbed his sleep. Hew was not in the habit of thinking about girls. He had given up on them since most of those he knew, the sisters of his fellow officers or friends of his own sister, despised the poverty that had forced him to rise up through the ranks of his regiment rather than buy his captaincy as people of his class found it more convenient to do. If Hew showed any romantic interest in such girls, they smirked and pouted and made him feel very uncomfortable. Alice made him feel uncomfortable too, but in quite a different way. He wanted her to like him. He wanted that very much. And if a girl such as her could steal a head, surely he could hide it. Moreover, although Hew was a staunch supporter of King George and the colonel was a traitor, what harm could his head do now? It was only proper that it should be reunited with the body and left in peace.

However, before he could do anything at all with the wig bag, Major Slavering stamped up, dragging the Duke of Mimsdale behind him. For one terrible moment Hew thought the major had also realized that Alice and Dan had been empty-handed as they galloped away. But the major was too busy cursing to think of anything. Hew stuffed the last of the sheets into the basket and slammed it shut. "Nothing more here," he said firmly. "Shall we let the laundryman go?"

"I don't give a farthing about the laundryman, Captain Ffrench, but we'll keep his cankerous cart until we have delivered this sniveling aristocrat to the Fleet prison.' Slavering was jabbing at the Duke of Mimsdale's shins with his scabbard, making the poor man dance. He was determined to take something from the whole fiasco and imprisoning the duke seemed the most satisfactory option. After a day or two with only rats for company, His Great Gormless Graceness would most certainly pay handsomely for his release. The laundryman slithered up, whining about the money owed to him. Major Slavering batted him aside and the man scurried off, shouting that he lived by the Thames and if pony, cart, and laundry did not appear and soon, he would complain to the king himself.

The duke was silent and gloomy as he was bundled on top of the basket to endure the short but extremely humiliating journey. At the Fleet, the warden was very happy indeed to meet him and soon he and Major Slavering were engrossed in highly important discussions of a financial nature.

Waved peremptorily away by the major, Hew prodded the pony. At first, he aimed straight down toward the river, as would have been expected, but once out of sight of the prison he turned west. It took about an hour to reach the poorest part of Chelsea, far beyond the big houses with gardens, where Hew's mother lived in a dwelling so modest that its walls seemed too embarrassed to stand up straight. He jumped down and knocked on the door. "Mother?" he called. "Mother, are you in?"

A lady wearing a darned cap and gown appeared. "Hew! I wasn't expecting you." She was all smiles, but her brown eyes, so like her son's, were anxious. "Come in, come in," she said. Then she saw the pony and laughed. It was a nice sound and the pony looked hopefully for a treat. "My dear boy, have you swapped Marron for this, and your captaincy for life as washer-woman?"

Hew grinned. Just hearing his mother's voice eased the knots from his shoulders. "It's a bit of a story," he said, jumping back onto the wagon, unstrapping the basket and rummaging about. "I can't stop, but—" The wig bag appeared.

His mother looked surprised. "You've brought me a wig?" she exclaimed. "Bless me, Hew, won't I just be in the forefront of fashion now?"

Hew looked a little rueful. "I'm sorry, Mother," he said. "It's not actually a wig, or a present for you at all."

She appeared crestfallen, then, when Hew looked contrite, shook her head so that the ribbons on her cap fluttered. "I'm only teasing, my darling," she said. "What on earth would I do with a wig, except sell it, I suppose."

"Are things bad at the moment?" Hew frowned. He wanted to help his mother, but most of his pay still went to settle his father's gambling debts and to refund the money he had borrowed to buy his horse.

"Never mind about that now," said Mrs Ffrench. "Tell me about this mysterious wig bag that contains neither wig nor present."

Hew jumped down and threw the reins over a tree stump before following his mother inside. The cramped hall was drab, but the parlor bore traces of a once elegant life, with furniture obviously brought from a house rather less cramped. Hew looked around, hesitated, then bundled all the clothes out of his mother's workbasket and tucked the wig bag into the bottom. However, before replacing all the mending, on impulse he opened the wig bag up and glanced inside. For a second or two he was revolted. Uncle Frank's head was not a cozy sight, but then he paused and the two men stared gravely at each other. The colonel's expression, ruefully grateful, made Hew smile at first, then the little hairs on the back of his neck stood on end. This was most certainly not the expression that had been on the dead man's face when he was on Temple Bar. Of that Hew was sure. He looked again, but Uncle Frank's expression remained the same. He even had a twinkle in his eye. Now, as a sensible person, Hew knew this to be quite impossible. Nevertheless, he tied the bag up smartly and covered it over. "There," he said. "Can you keep this in here for me?"

"I can," said his mother, wanting to be accommodating, "but I would like to know what is in it."

"I can't tell you," said Hew, taking her hands, from which, he noticed, all the rings were now gone, "and really, it's best if you don't know. Absolutely best."

A look passed between them. They understood each other well, for Hew had been his mother's main support on the many evenings when his father had returned home from the races, drunkenly raging about the failure of horses he had bought with other people's money. After he was killed in a pointless duel, Mrs. Ffrench had been deluged with unsettled bills and had sold everything to pay them. Now she scraped a living making and mending gloves, dresses, and hats, while Hew's sister, Mabel, was a governess to the young daughters of the Duke of Cantankering in Lincoln's Inn Fields. There, at least, was good news, for Mabel's employer liked her and, to Mrs. Ffrench's hopeful delight, Mabel was being gently courted by the Cantankering's oldest son, Peregrine, Marquis of Trotting. During her many lonely evenings, Mrs. Ffrench prayed that the match would be made and that Mabel would be saved from turning into the sour old maid she was threatening to become. The only worry here was that Peregrine seemed too shy to propose. It would be the last straw if this came to nothing.

Hew knew all about his mother's ambitions for his sister and a sudden panic engulfed him. What was he doing? If Uncle Frank's head was discovered here, everything would be lost. He was a thoroughly bad son and a thoroughly bad brother. At that moment he came within a whisker of grabbing the wig bag, running out the door, and throwing Uncle Frank into the river.

But he did not. Instead, he remembered Uncle Frank's look and Alice's face and led his mother to a chair. "You mustn't know the contents, Mother," he said, "and please never look. The wig bag isn't stolen, if that's what you are thinking. It belongs to somebody—" He did not know quite how to describe Alice, but opted for "an acquaintance." His mother opened her mouth, but Hew rushed on. "Yes, I know it sounds odd, Mother, but it belongs to a girl I met and, as soon as I can, I want to return it to her, or at least get it to her family, who I think live in the north.

But in the meantime, I didn't know what else to do with it so I brought it here."

"Can't you keep it at the barracks?"

"No. If Major Slavering found it, well . . ." Hew trailed off.

Mrs. Ffrench looked at her workbasket. "It will be safe here," she said, not wanting to push Hew any further, for though she was curious, she trusted him implicitly. "Now, Mabel brought back the end of a veal pie from Lincoln's Inn Fields yesterday. The Cantankerings may not pay much but they are very generous with food." Her jaw tightened a little, for she did not like accepting charity. "I'll get you a slice."

Hew shook his head and headed for the door. "I must be off at once," he said, but after a few moments he returned. His mother was standing just where he had left her. "Here," he said, and handed her a pair of soiled and torn stockings and three pairs of large gloves with M initialed on each. "If anybody asks, you can say that I brought these for you to wash and mend because they got damaged this morning in a scuffle. You don't need to know any more than that." Then he kissed his mother warmly on both cheeks and hurried out.

He was glad to find that the pony knew his own way back to his riverside home and, when the laundryman appeared, he gave him sixpence as well as telling him to do the laundry in double-quick time. The laundryman humphed and wanted to make Hew listen to all his complaints, but Hew did not wait. Quite suddenly, having put his mother in such danger on her behalf, he found he wanted to discover more about Alice Towneley than her cornflower eyes, so instead of returning straight to the barracks, he made his way at speed back to Grosvenor Square. There he waited until a girl appeared, sent out by Ursula to pick up a cordial for her nerves.

Using a smile and a soldier's easy charm, it was not hard to get the girl to talk. Alice's family, he discovered, lived at Towneley Hall and were "real rich and real grand." "In fact," the girl said, flattered by Hew's attention, "if she weren't a papist and didn't 'ave such a wicked temper, I'm sure she could 'ave married a prince." Hew revealed nothing, but after he had doffed the new hat he had had to buy after his trip up Temple Bar and left her, his face was grave. What a bonehead he was. If Alice's family were rich and grand, she was obviously quite out of the league of a humble captain. When he thought of Uncle Frank sitting in his mother's work basket, he felt hot all over and walked faster and faster, trying to decide the best thing to do. By the time he got back to the barracks, he had made up his mind. He could not leave Alice entirely in the lurch, so he would do the honorable thing and get the colonel's head to Towneley. After that, he would leave England and seek active service in France.

7

From behind a tree, Dan watched Hew and the servant girl. After stealing a chunk of ham from a butcher's basket and wolfing it down in a style that he knew was not one employed at the sort of dinner tables Alice frequented, he too had returned to the environs of Grosvenor Square, not knowing where else to begin tracing the whereabouts of Uncle Frank. He was glad to have found Hew so easily and, as he followed him, an idea began to form in his head, which, he believed, was easily as daring as any idea of Alice's. The thought that she would be impressed was very pleasing. Dan's plan was this. Nobody questioned a uniform. If Dan and Alice could dress up as members of Kingston's Light Horse, they could travel unmolested, even carrying a wig bag with a head in it. They already had the requisite black horses with their regulation docked tails. If they also wore the red coat, yellow sash, and gloves, who would dare stop them? When Hew began to walk more quickly, it entirely suited Dan's mood, for he found himself full of a kind of excitement he had never felt before, not even as he raised the ax for his first execution, and that had been exciting enough.

The more Dan thought, the better his plan seemed to be, especially as—and he stopped to slap his thigh—*the barracks were also the place that Uncle Frank was most likely to be!* By Dan's calculation, Slavering would have searched the laundry basket, found the wig bag, looked inside it, and was probably even now encouraging all those ignorant troopers to mock the poor colonel and stick silly hats on his head. When Hew disappeared through the gates, however, Dan was brought up short. How could he get inside? He slipped behind a cutler's stall crushed hard up against the walls and scrutinized the place carefully.

Between the rough stone pillars that marked the entrance, the double gates opened and shut constantly as men and horses flowed in and out. Dan did not have to wait long before a group of blacksmiths, brawny men like Dan himself, walked boldly up to the guardhouse and demanded entry. Dan clasped his hands together. He would not get a better chance than this. The cutler was deep in conversation with a customer, so Dan took the opportunity to steal several knives and three pairs of scissors. These he wrapped in an expensive linen apron and bulked them out with the cutler's walking stick and the iron bar he used to ward off thieving boys. If not inspected too closely, the bundle could have been full of blacksmiths' tools. Dan's conscience twinged, but he settled it by blaming his new dishonesty on Alice. With his bundle neatly secured, he quickly caught up with the blacksmiths and walked boldly through the gates with them.

The horses that needed shoeing were standing sleepily in the yard and the troopers who held them had discarded their coats and opened their shirts to give their armpits an airing. Dan's heart sank as he realized that the blacksmiths had to wait in line, in full view of everybody, to be allocated an animal. He had thought that once inside the barracks it would be easy to disappear. Worse, the line moved swiftly and in a moment he found himself holding a horse. He gazed at it, for he had little practical knowledge of blacksmithery. He bent down and picked up a foot. He could manage that. He felt the shoe. It was loose. He let the foot drop and began slowly to open his bundle.

But before he had even undone the string, he was hit smartly from behind by a stocky oaf with a boxer's face, a cauliflower ear, and two mighty fists. "I saw you slippin' into our line," the oaf said threateningly.

"You must be a foreigner from over the river." He punched Dan right on his wounded shoulder. "Well, I live round 'ere and I say this 'oss is mine. Go and find yourself another. This lot's new shoes means new shoes for my brats. Now get lost." Dan tried to look gruff and quarrelsome. He even pretended to square off. One of the troopers ran over and clicked his tongue. He didn't want trouble. "Just get on with it," he said, shrugging at Dan and nodding at the smaller man.

Dan picked up his bundle and moved away. He strolled aimlessly for a bit, then, when the air was full of the clank and hiss of a dozen blacksmiths hard at work, he walked through an arch, down a cobbled passageway, past three sets of stalls, and into a flagged harness room. He moved swiftly. If anybody challenged him, he would say he was a chef looking for the kitchens.

The harness store was filled with bridles and saddles, and underneath the pegs lurked a dozen or so pairs of enormous boots. Dan suddenly saw the first flaw in his plan. Alice was so slight. The uniform of even the smallest trooper would drown her. He frowned, then he heard noises behind him and made for the door. He was too late to get out and two troopers pushed passed him. They barely looked at him. Dan relaxed a little, even nodding to them as he moved on. He must keep calm. At the far end of the next room was a small stone staircase that Dan climbed to find himself in a dormitory. Uniforms were all over the place here, some folded neatly, some heaped in piles. Even better, the troopers on the bunks were all fast asleep. Tiptoeing across, Dan held a coat against himself. It was much too small for a man of his girth so he threw it down and picked up another, and another and another, until he found a reasonable fit. As he stripped, one of the sleeping beauties gurgled and rolled over, waking another, who sat up and threw a boot before covering his own head with a blanket. Dan stood, half in and half out of his new britches, until the snores were regular again. Then he pulled on the rest of the uniform and rolled his own clothes in with his knives and scissors. He had only just time to cram a hat onto his head and seize a sword before he heard laughing and stamping on the stairs and the room was filled with soldiers returning from their shift. Some looked at him curiously, and one or two were puzzled, for they could not place him, but before any could speak Dan made for the door. It was as he ran down the steps that he bumped flat into Hew himself. Only the shadows saved Dan from instant recognition.

"What are you doing in full uniform, trooper?" Hew asked sharply, for he had not heard that the men in barracks were to be ordered out and hoped this did not herald bad news about any sighting of Alice.

"I'm, er, I've got to go and see the general," Dan replied, trying to imply that his business was too urgent to brook any interruption. Hew would have pressed him further had not a commotion in the yard distracted him. One of the horses wasn't happy. "Very well, then," he said. "About your business."

"Sir." Dan was not sure if he was meant to touch his hat or not, so he simply lifted his arm a little and carried on down the steps.

"The general's not down there," came Hew's voice. "He's up in his quarters."

Dan stopped. "Thank you, sir," he said, and had to turn around and pass Hew again. Fortunately, Hew's attention was already elsewhere. Nevertheless, he did not leave until he had seen Dan disappear.

The first floor was very comfortable, with rugs, hangings, and armchairs. The general was nowhere to be seen. Dan hesitated, wondering if Hew would still be lurking, but before he could tiptoe down to see, he heard somebody approaching. Losing his cool completely, he rushed toward a small door set in an alcove. It was unlocked and Dan tumbled through. This room was in the most awful mess, with clothes scattered all over the beds. Dan hid, then, when nobody came in after him, picked up some of the items, and, even though his pulse was racing, grinned. God was really smiling! The general had sons and the boys had obviously been given Kingston's uniforms as fancy dress. Here was stuff that might just fit Alice. Yanking up the corners of a blanket, so that everything—shirts, breeches, sashes, gloves, stockings, boots, coats, hats, and swords—dumped into the middle, Dan was thinking perfectly clearly again. If no bits of uniform remained for either boy, it would be assumed that the servants had put them away. It would be hours before anybody suspected they had been stolen. He knotted the blanket and hung it over his shoulder, opened the door a crack, and found himself confronted directly not only by the general's back but by the regimental cat.

The cat gave a loud meow and, before Dan could stop it, wedged itself between the door and the doorpost. The general half-turned, bent down, and waggled his fingers. "Kitty, kitty, kitty," he cooed. Dan willed the cat to move, but it only arched at him and purred. "Go on back to your kittens, then, kitty, kitty, kitty." The general's tone was sickly sweet, but Dan knew this was reserved strictly for animals. When addressing humans, it was lethal. He reversed at high speed. Just as he reached the window, his blanket sack began to move. At first the movements were so small Dan hardly felt them, but as the cat in the doorway's purr grew louder, so the movements in the blanket grew stronger, and even through his uniform coat he felt tiny claws scratching. Gods alive! The cat must have made a nest for the kittens on the bed and he had swept them all up. The door was pushed wider. The general was coming in. He stopped short when he saw Dan. "I say," he began.

Dan did not wait to hear any more but smashed the window and leaped. The drop was not huge and he landed safely on the roof above the horses' stalls. The crashing and splintering seemed ear-splitting and one of the boys' boots escaped, thumping slowly over the slates before teetering and toppling into the dungheap steaming gently below. Dan was flat on his back and, before he could get up, he felt a small, neat weight land on his chest. The cat, in pursuit of her kittens, had leaped after him. Dan tried to push her away, but she insisted on clinging to him, cross now, for her kittens were wailing. Two or three white faces, cute as could be, peered out of the blanket. The bravest emerged and wanted to play. Framed by jagged glass, the general was looking down, too astonished to shout—yet.

Dan knew he had only a few seconds. Pulling as many kittens from his bundle as he could find, he plucked the cat from his shirt and, grabbing everything else, ran to the edge of the roof and jumped again.

The landing in the dungheap was foul, but although Dan sank up to his armpits it was at least soft—and he had kept hold of the bundle. Something surprised him, though. The heat was intense, for the middle of a well-made dungheap is hot as an oven, and the Kingston's men prided themselves on being able to cook potatoes in theirs. It was quite impossible to stay still. Not that this mattered. The general's head had disappeared. He was not wasting time shouting. He was on his way down.

With great difficulty, for the dungheap was keen to suck him under, Dan clambered and clawed his way out and ran straight into the stables. They were full of men grooming or lounging on the water barrels and when they saw him they roared with laughter. "Fell into the muck heap," Dan called, and sped out the other side. There was no time to rinse himself under the pump and he still didn't have Uncle Frank. "Surely missy'll understand," he told himself as he slid around the feed room, leaving smelly brown splashes in his wake. He could hear the general's voice and slowed down, forcing himself to break cover and march casually across the yard. He would be done for if he couldn't get out but he must not, *must not,* look like a man in a panic. Settling his bundle more firmly under his arm and with a face as red as a beetroot, he managed a jaunty wave at the sentry, who, only vaguely aware of the hullabaloo, saluted. As Dan passed through the gate, he copied the sentry's actions and saluted back. No mean feat, he thought as he finally allowed himself to run, for a hangman whose boots are filled with manure.

It was evening by the time he got back to Alice and before he could say much at all she collapsed into furious tears. He had been away far too long. What did he mean, he had been messing about with kittens? She had been frantic with worry. And she was starving. Eventually, Dan stopped speaking. It wasn't worth it because she wasn't listening. He let her shout and bawl. It seemed easier.

He was no longer in his Kingston's uniform, having changed out of it by a stream and attempted to wash it. He had also stolen some loaves from a baker's windowsill and produced a loaf now, watching as Alice, with a small hiccup, grabbed it and crammed it into her mouth.

"You'll be sick if you eat like that," he observed. "Nonsense," she mumbled, spraying crumbs. "I'm never sick."

"You were sick at Colonel Towneley's execution," he reminded her.

"That was different." She wolfed down a bit more, then had to take a breather. "This is so fresh. Just like we get at home. Uncle Frank could eat a whole loaf at once, although not without butter." She stopped chewing. "You've got more than his head in that bundle, Dan Skinslicer." With bread in her stomach, Alice felt much better and was prepared to be nicer.

Dan braced himself. "I'm afraid I never found Uncle Frank," he said, and blocked his ears as the tirade began again. She went on and on, and on and on some more, but by the time she cried her final "So now what are we going to do?" the response was a gentle snore. Dan had fallen asleep where he sat.

Alice shut her mouth with a snap. He was hopeless. She would never, never have returned without Uncle Frank. There must have been a way to find him. She grumbled to herself and, deliberately not waiting until Dan woke up, ripped open the bundle with bad grace. However, as she unwrapped the uniforms and found the swords, her muttering ceased and her bad temper began to dissolve. She had not been entirely fair. Poor Dan had, after all, walked miles and his booty, she had to admit, was really very splendid. They would be two dragoons together. She ate another loaf of bread more slowly and thoughtfully before she lay down. Dan was clever after all. She would tell him so in the morning.

She didn't, because they were both stiff and grumpy. Then she couldn't help giggling as Dan squeezed himself into his uniform because, in truth, the breeches were at least one size too small. "They looked well enough in the barracks," Dan said resentfully when he eventually managed to do them up. Alice, however, was soon perfectly attired from top to toe and Dan was invited to admire her dashing looks as she bound up her hair under her hat and buckled on her sword. "There," she exclaimed, shaking the grass seeds out of Marron's tail. "I'd fool even Captain Ffrench."

"I dare say," said Dan drily, pushing his feet unwillingly back into his boots. Even though the manure was gone, the memory of it, along with more than a faint whiff, would take a long time to banish. "Now, let's head north."

Alice stopped prancing about. "North?" she queried. "Oh no, Dan, we're going back into London. I told you. We can't go north without Uncle Frank."

"Don't be foolish now," said Dan, his expression darkening. "You've done your very best. The colonel knows how brave you are. You don't have to prove anything to him. We'll go north and, when you are safe at home, I promise I will come back. Who knows, maybe your father can do something."

"But I want to take Uncle Frank home myself." Alice could feel her voice rising like a child's and didn't like it. But really, who was Dan to tell her what to do? If he had failed to get Uncle Frank, she certainly wouldn't. Rolling up her discarded skirts and tying them behind the saddle, she mounted. "Are you coming or not?" she asked, trying to pretend she didn't care either way.

Dan climbed clumsily on to the major's horse. "I'm going where you are going," he said, his mouth set, "but we're both going north."

"You don't have to come with me." Alice jammed her hat more firmly onto her head and aimed Marron south. "But whatever you say, I am going to get Uncle Frank. The uniform you so kindly brought will be quite enough protection." Her politeness was like the prick of a needle.

Dan pushed Belter in front of Marron and tried to make the horse turn. "The uniform will not make you invisible," he said. "If they look close, they'll see at once who you are." He dug Belter harder in the ribs and gave her a sideways look. "If that happens, you know, Captain Ffrench will certainly be questioned. Major Slavering will have guessed by now that it was him who gave us time to get out of your granny's window."

Alice flushed, but still did not hesitate. Indeed, she just sat up a little taller and wondered how well the uniform suited her. "Good-bye, then, Dan Skinslicer," she said, urging Marron into a trot. "I'm sure my father will give you a good welcome and I'll follow on as soon as I can."

Dan swore loudly and, thinking to teach Alice a lesson, tried to leave her. But Belter was reluctant, then downright pig-headed, and whipped around to catch up with his friend. When Dan appeared, unwillingly, alongside her, Alice gave him the one-raised-eyebrow treatment. But Dan did not smile and, as they rode along, his face looked even more like a cobblestone than usual.

It was at least half an hour before Alice broke the silence. "If you try to stand in your stirrups, then fall naturally, then stand again, you will soon be able to rise to the trot and be much more comfortable," she said, trying to sound conciliatory rather than smug. "John, our head groom, taught me that when I first started to ride."

Dan sniffed. Alice gave up, but when she next looked over, Dan's broad forehead was red under his three-cornered hat and his cheeks were puffing as he bounced. "Glory be," he burst out at last, "this must be worse than being at sea."

The frost was broken. Alice gave him her most captivating smile.

"Do you always get your own way?" Dan asked after Alice had shown him how to hold the reins properly and what his legs were for.

"Usually," she admitted, quite unperturbed by the implied criticism, "but I'm always very nice about it." Dan shook his head, but he could not help grinning. Alice looked at him and nodded approvingly. "You're quite a stylish rider, Dan Skinslicer," she said. "When we've got Uncle Frank's head, we'll make excellent time home."

Dan grunted. "Maybe we won't find it."

But Alice tossed her hair. "We will find it," she said, and, as if to underline her certainty, kicked Marron into a canter.

It was not long before they saw some troopers dressed similarly to themselves and, catching them up, they fell in right at the back. Nobody questioned them, for unfamiliar dragoons were often appearing, replacing those lost at the battle of Culloden earlier in the year. Some of the men spoke to Dan, and he, with a native cunning he was fast picking up from Alice, confided that his slim companion was the young son of a high-ranking officer and had been entrusted to him to look after. "Best not to speak to him," Dan whispered. "He's a right snotty-nosed little fop." Alice never knew why the troopers avoided her, but Dan smiled a tiny smile to himself and settled back in his saddle. Just before the barracks, he and Alice peeled off. Nobody bade them good-bye. Nobody even saw them go.

Inside the barracks, Major Slavering had not slept well. As more and more of his crack troops straggled in empty-handed, with no news at all of Alice, Dan, or the two stolen horses, his temper grew shorter and shorter. "Call yourselves soldiers," he stormed as the men stood in the mustering yard, tired and disconsolate, wanting only a decent breakfast. "How can a couple of cranks carrying a head have got past you?"

There was muttering among the troopers and one took his courage in his hands. "When we chased the two villains around Grosvenor Square," he said, nervous but buoyed up by his fellows, "we didn't see no 'ead."

"Of course you didn't," replied the major, eyeballing the unfortunate soldier. "They'd have wrapped it in something. Dangling heads from saddles went out some time ago. Is that not so, Captain Ffrench? You are the educated one among us." Hew was standing behind the major. "How would *you* think they are carrying it?"

Hew cleared his throat. "I imagine in a cloak or something," he said.

The major looked more closely at him. "Did you see anything containing a head when that traitorous couple made their escape?"

"No, Major, I didn't," said Hew, "but maybe one of them was holding it on the side away from me."

"Perhaps." Slavering scrutinized his captain. Hew's dark eyes were so irritatingly honest. But now they seemed to have some kind of veil over them, a veil that told Slavering, as clear as a public announcement, that Hew was harboring a secret. Ever since Alice's unexpected catapulting from the ladder, the major had entertained doubts about his captain's commitment to bringing the girl to justice and it seemed more than curious that whenever Alice vanished, Hew was in the vicinity. Slavering walked forward until his face was only an inch from Hew's nose. "If that girl and her accomplice were not carrying the head," he said slowly, brushing an imaginary spot of dirt from Hew's shoulder, "perhaps they have left it in that house in Grosvenor Square where, I believe, the grandmother and aunt live. Should we conduct a thorough search and bring the two ladies here to question them? Ladies like that can't be so very hard to break."

Hew did not allow himself to flinch but, behind his back, one hand formed a fist. "We could go and search the house, if you like," he said evenly, "but if the girl did leave the colonel's head—"

"The traitor's head," the major hissed, standing so close to Hew that their buttons touched.

"The head." Hew would make no further concession. "If they did leave it in Grosvenor Square, I'm sure the two ladies will know nothing about it. One is extremely old—I'm told the king believes she is the oldest person in London—and the other is, well, certainly eccentric." The effect was as Hew hoped. The reference to the king was enough to have the major step backward. Nobody wanted to fall afoul of the king. It was safe to tease and misuse the unpopular Duke of Mimsdale, but Lady Widdrington was a riskier target.

Slavering paced up and down. "That laundry basket," he said abruptly. "You returned it to the laundryman?"

Hew didn't blink. "I did, sir."

"Did you look inside it?"

Hew had rehearsed this to himself already. "I didn't need to. It had already been half-emptied by you and what was left in it flew out with the two escapees. I simply put everything back in as best I could. It will still be with the laundryman. If you have any doubts, sir, I will take you to him and you can see for yourself." Hew made as if to sidestep the major and give appropriate orders, but Slavering stopped him and his look was sly.

"Too lowly a task for you, Captain Ffrench." He barked at the men. "I want two volunteers to go to the river right now, find this laundry person, and bring him here. I'll talk to him personally. We'll soon find that head. It must have left its mark somewhere."

It was an hour before the laundryman appeared and by that time the troops were restless. The laundryman himself had only one idea, and that was to please the major, who kept running his hand up and down the blade of his sword in a way that made the skin creep. Yet the laundryman could only swear on his life that neither he nor his wife had found anything strange in the duke's linen and certainly no traces of a head at all. When the major finally dismissed him, the laundryman was so grateful he could not stop bowing and sniveling. "A man like yourself will certainly be in need of a good laundry service," he groveled. "Me and the wife, we're as quick as quick. Why, we only got the duke's laundry yesterday as the bells chimed four and he will get it back before sunset today."

Major Slavering stopped in his tracks. "Four, you say? Four o'clock? Are you sure?" He seized the laundry-man's collar.

"Yes, sir, sure, sir, absolutely, sir," the man gushed as best he could with his neck squeezed so hard.

Slavering dropped him and turned to Hew. His triumph was absolute. "Four, eh?" he said, and the lightness in his voice was more ominous than any bark. "And you said this man was easy to find? Not so easy, apparently, since you left the Fleet prison long before four. Did you, perhaps, make some stops with that heavy basket on the way, Captain Ffrench? Now, let me recall." He crossed his arms. "Oh yes. Don't you have a mother and a sister living somewhere in Chelsea? Maybe you paid them a visit?" He tapped Hew's nose. "A visit 'a-head' of your usual one on a Sunday, if you'll forgive the pun?"

Hew went green with dismay but knew at once that he must come clean. "I did pay them a visit," he admitted. "Some of the duke's laundry got damaged in the scuffles and my mother sews. The stuff is valuable, so it seemed prudent to get it mended. I mean, you never know when the duke will be back in favor at court again and these dukes can make a terrible fuss over anything—even a nightcap."

The troopers sniggered. The nightcap would live long in their memories.

At once Hew knew that mentioning the nightcap had been a mistake. "BE QUIET!" the major yelled. Then he turned back to Hew. "I think we will pay your mother a visit, Captain Two-Effs, just to make sure all that prudent mending is safe." His veins pulsed. "Bring horses for the captain and myself, and you two"—he kicked out at two dragoons standing, gawping—"get your own animals and accompany us."

The major rode at full speed to Chelsea, scattering beggars as he went. Hew followed behind, a sickness in his stomach, cursing everything. It wasn't Alice's fault, of course, but if she had never attempted to rescue the colonel's head, he would never have met her. All the way to Chelsea, he made a frantic list of people to whom he might appeal once Uncle Frank's head was discovered. The best person would be the Duke of Cantankering. Although Cantankering's relationship with King George could never be relied on and the ensuing scandal would certainly mean that Lord Trotting would no longer marry Mabel, the duke was still Hew's best hope. Anything to prevent his mother from being thrown into jail at the mercy of men worse even than Major Slavering.

As they neared Mrs. Ffrench's door, Hew tried to go ahead, but the major was having none of it. "I never had you down as a mommy's boy," he jeered, pushing Hew back. Their boots were splashed by a pig scuffling through a puddle and the major roared his disgust.

"For all your fancy two-effed name, this is not a part of London frequented by gentlewomen. Those jokes the troopers tell about Mr. F-f-french being a g-gambler and a d-debtor are obviously true."

Hew pressed his legs harder into his horse's flanks. He could not afford to lose his temper. All he could do was mutter to himself that no gentleman would use his father's reputation as a way of insulting his mother. But then Slavering was not a gentleman. That's what made him dangerous.

Mrs. Ffrench opened the front door before the major could wallop it, thus slightly wrong-footing him. "Major Slavering, I presume?" she asked, glad that she was wearing a clean cap and her least darned gown. Her house might be small and the area discreditable, but Major Slavering should see that she had not forgotten her manners. "Hew." She moved forward to kiss her son. "I'm not sure to what I owe this honor."

The major could feel the back of his neck bristling. How was it possible to sound so superior with a greeting? "There is no honor, madam," he said. "I have reason to believe that you have in your possession something that does not belong to you. That's all."

"I have many things here which do not belong to me," said Mrs. Ffrench easily. "As you probably know from Hew, I take in sewing. I have some at present. That does not belong to me. But then neither," she added, "does it belong to you."

"We'll see about that, shall we?" growled the major. He and the troopers thrust their way into the little house, leaving Hew and his mother to bring up the rear.

"Mabel's in the parlour," said Mrs. Ffrench. "She's come to fetch her things and say good-bye because she's going north with the Cantankerings for a month or so tomorrow." Hew squeezed his mother's hand. There was nothing else to do.

When the major encountered Mabel, his eyes gleamed and he bowed ostentatiously low. Mabel, who had passed him occasionally when she had watched Hew parading the dragoons, ignored him, and Mrs. Ffrench hastened over to stand by her daughter.

The major insolently examined the contents of the room before beginning, with solemn effrontery, to open the drawers and doors of the single cabinet and cupboard, dropping the contents onto the floor. As the china smashed, Hew started forward, but his mother restrained him. "Let the major find what he has come for and then leave us in peace," she said, keeping her voice very relaxed, "but I must say that it would help, Major Slavering, if I knew exactly what it was that you sought."

The major glared at her. "I'm looking for a head, ma'am."

Mrs. Ffrench jumped, but Mabel began to laugh. "A head?" she asked. "Why, Major, you don't look as if you have lost yours quite yet."

Slavering glowered and ordered the two troopers to search the bedrooms. Bangs and crashes marked their progress through the three small upstairs chambers. Mabel's face was livid but, to Hew's relief, although her temper was obviously simmering, at least it was simmering quietly.

The troopers emerged empty-handed. At once Major Slavering began to look about the parlor more carefully, running his hands down the walls and even getting one trooper to stick an arm up the chimney. Nothing.

Hew moved forward, trying not to look at the workbasket. "I think you have disturbed my mother long enough," he said coldly.

But the major was not finished. Slowly, quite deliberately and tortuously slowly it seemed to Hew, he finally turned his attention to Mrs. Ffrench's mending. He walked round the basket a few times, even gave it a poke or two, then, quite suddenly, kicked it over. As the contents spilled out, the wig bag rolled into the middle of the floor with a dull thud. Hew did not dare look at his mother.

Slavering's whole face changed. A wig bag. *A wig bag!* Of course! Oh, how excellently clever! What better place to hide a head? He gave it a poke with his foot and guffawed. Then he bent down to open it. The ribbon was knotted and not easily undone. In the end, using Mrs. Ffrench's scissors, he snipped it and, plunging both hands inside, seized a clump of hair and pulled. Hew closed his eyes and swayed slightly. He opened them just in time to see the major clutching a black wig and staring at it in disbelief. Hew felt as though the world had stopped. Slavering dropped the wig, peered down, and plunged his hand in again. This time he brought out a carved wooden head, the sort wigmakers use as models. This he tossed on top of the wig before plunging in again and again, bringing out rope upon rope of horsehair, each rope grayer and greasier than the last. Finally, he picked up the bag itself and shook it so hard that his epaulets thumped up and down. It was only then that he accepted that the bag was absolutely and completely empty.

Hew was now deathly pale but Mrs. Ffrench's composure never faltered. "Have you quite finished?" she asked in voice far too ordinary for the occasion. "I think you have caused enough damage. I am fixing the lining of that wig. It belongs to one of the king's cousins. The king himself sent it."

The major was hopping with rage. He had been beaten for now and he well knew it. "We live in treacherous times, ma'am." He ground out the words through his teeth, his fury almost uncontrollable. "Two traitors escaped when your son was supposed to have them cornered. If we have been a trouble to you, you should blame him. Now I'll bid you good day. Come, Captain Ffrench. We've wasted enough time here." With that, he stamped out and Hew had no choice but to follow.

When the door slammed, Mabel began to get up but her mother shook her head. They waited five whole minutes and Mrs. Ffrench inspected the house front and back before she finally sank down in her chair. "I suppose that was one good thing to come out of your father's hopeless life," she said. "I learned that people who want something you don't give them often leave a spy behind. Anyway, I think we are all clear now."

Mabel humphed and shifted her skirts, under which, neatly wrapped in a white pillowcase, was the unmistakable shape of Uncle Frank's head. "It was lucky you didn't obey Hew's instructions not to open that beastly wig bag, Mother," she said. "Just fancy if you hadn't."

"Oh," said Mrs. Ffrench, settling her cap straight with hands that were not quite steady, "I saw those uniforms at the end of the street from the upstairs window and I just knew that wig bag must be responsible. I must say, though, Mabel dear, I hardly expected a head, but, frankly, the man's expression when I pulled him out was so beseeching that it was not really too much to wrap him in a pillowcase." She gave Mabel a watery smile. "I hope the pillow-case will survive. At least it's used to heads, I sup-pose, even if they are usually snoring rather than dead." It was a pathetic joke, but it was all Mrs. Ffrench could manage.

"Oh, I expect it will be none the worse for wear," said Mabel crisply, staring at the lump in front of her. For all her bravado, she found she really did not want to pick Uncle Frank up. Mrs. Ffrench saw Mabel's expression and, trying not to hesitate herself, grasped the pillowcase, unfolded it, and propped the head on the floor while she made the wig bag comfortable for it once again. She tidied the horsehair and was just cutting a piece of new ribbon when she glanced at Uncle Frank and screamed loudly. Mabel leaped at once onto a chair. "What is it?" she cried.

"Nothing, nothing." Her mother calmed herself. "The poor man winked at me. That's all. It is probably just the muscles in the eye sockets beginning to deteriorate. Nothing else. Really," she added, trying to be perfectly matter-of-fact, "the head looks very cheerful, all things considered, and the pitch has preserved it very well." Nevertheless, she quickly dropped Uncle Frank back onto his horsehair berth and tied up the ribbon in a double bow. Whatever happened, she did not wish to be winked at again. "Now we have to decide what to do with him."

"Well, whoever he is—was—I don't think he should remain here," said Mabel. "Major Slavering could return." She thought for a moment. "Maybe I should take him to Lincoln's Inn Fields, then slip him in with the Cantankerings' baggage tomorrow. At least he will be out of London, which will be best for everybody. When we can, we'll let Hew know what we've done and make some arrangement to get the wretched thing to where it is supposed to be going. I really think that's what we should do, Mother, don't you?"

Her mother looked worried but nodded. She didn't like involving Mabel in all this skulduggery, but it did seem a sensible suggestion. Mabel, braver now, put the wig bag back in the workbasket. "Goodness, how heavy it is!" she exclaimed. "What a clever man he must have been! All those brains!" Her mother did not look amused. Mabel changed the subject. "Aren't you curious, Mother, about the mystery girl Hew spoke of?"

"Very," said Mrs. Ffrench, "but Hew only said that she lives in the north. I could tell she meant something to him, though. She must," she added as an afterthought, "or he would never have risked our lives by bringing that head here."

"Which he had absolutely no business to do, girl or not!" exclaimed Mabel, cross at her mother's indulgence.

"Don't be horrid, Mabel."

"I'm not being horrid, Mother, but Hew should have thought."

Mrs. Ffrench sighed. Her daughter was always so quick to judge.

Mabel went back to the workbasket. "Now what are you doing?" cried Mrs. French, whose nerves were too frayed for any further excitement.

Mabel pulled the wig bag out and looked at it as if she might open it up and give Uncle Frank himself a telling-off. But she didn't. Instead, she headed for the stairs. "I'll have to move the head from the wig bag into a hatbox," she said, "because, while I do own a few hats, I don't own any wigs at all and it would be too dreadful if the Cantankering servants mistakenly delivered this to Lady Cantankering's room." Her lips twitched. "Although I'd love to see that woman come face-to-face with a head that is more attractive dead than hers is alive."

Mrs. Ffrench sighed. She hoped Mabel did not say such things to Lord Trotting. Then she fell to wondering again about Hew's friend. "A girl I met," he had said. But what kind of girl did you meet through mutual acquaintance with a head? The question was not one Mrs. Ffrench had ever expected to ask and so she was not surprised when she found herself quite unable to supply the answer.

If only Alice and Dan had been able to witness those scenes in Chelsea, much of what happened next would have been avoided. Still, Alice's determination to retrieve her uncle's head could not but lead to trouble, and trouble came quickly.

Since they had left the head outside the Duke of Mimsdale's house, it was there that Dan and Alice, having slipped away from the main body of the dragoons, first went. Their troopers' disguise was perfect and Alice held the horses while Dan knocked boldly on the front door to ask where the laundry basket had gone. The striking red-and-yellow uniform enhanced Dan's charms and the Mimsdale maidservant needed little persuasion to tell him everything he wanted to know.

"I'll keep the uniform once this escapade is over," Dan said to Alice. "That girl would never have looked at me in my real clothes."

Alice, as usual, tossed her head. "You can do better than a maidservant, Dan Skinslicer," she said.

Dan tossed his own head right back. "Maybe I don't want to." He remounted with a determined and not unbecoming bounce, enjoying Alice's discomfiture. "Now," he said, serious again, "the girl told me where to find the laundry basket, so we must hope the wig bag's still inside it and that the laundryman hasn't opened it." More confident of his horse, and conscious of the servant girl peeking at him from the kitchen window, he led the way out of Grosvenor Square. Alice followed but Dan did not like the look in her eye. "You and this horse are both laughing at me now," he accused her.

"Not at all," said Alice just a touch too demurely as she deliberately blocked the servant girl's view. "You sit very well and look very dashing. If I didn't know you were a hangman, I'd think you were an officer at least." Dan made a disbelieving face but swung along in finer style than ever before.

It was a bitter disappointment to both of them when the visit to the laundry drew a complete blank, but a relief to learn, through the laundryman's curses as he hopped up and down, bleating about persecution, that at least Major Slavering did not have Uncle Frank either.

"Somebody must have taken the wig bag out before it ever got here," Alice said as they rode away. "But who could it be and what would they have done with it?"

"Maybe Captain Ffrench took it," Dan suggested, and instantly regretted it, for Alice's face lit up. "Of course!" she exclaimed so loudly that people looked around.

"Now then, missy," Dan warned. "Keep quiet or you'll get us both arrested."

Alice brushed his worries aside. "We'll go to the barracks," she declared, "and follow Hew—I mean, Captain Ffrench. If he did save Uncle Frank's head from Major Slavering, he's bound to lead us to it sooner or later, and what's more, Dan Skinslicer, I'm sure he'll be only too delighted to hand it back."

"But," Dan pointed out, trying to dampen the sparkle in Alice's voice because he didn't like it, "I doubt he did save Uncle Frank, because if he got caught, he'd be dead meat. And why would he do it? Uncle Frank's nothing to him."

"He won't be caught," Alice stated after a small pause. "We've been lucky so far. Honestly, we only need to be lucky once more before we can get safely on the road to Towneley and be forgotten by everybody down here." She kicked Marron into a trot and Dan's horse, without bothering to wait for Dan's instructions, immediately followed suit.

They arrived at the barracks just in time to see Hew and Major Slavering returning from their trip to Chelsea in thunderous silence. Hew could think of nothing but the terrible fright his mother must have gotten when she had found Uncle Frank in the wig bag, and Slavering was so angry he could scarcely think at all.

Alice pushed Dan around the corner. "We'll just wait until Captain Ffrench comes out again," she whispered. But it was not until the morning that Hew emerged on yet another borrowed horse, and when Dan and Alice, having spent the night huddled under a wall, taking turns to keep watch, hauled themselves back onto their own horses, they had no idea where he was going.

Hew was heading straight to find Mabel. She would, by now, have returned to Lincoln's Inn Fields, and while Hew could not go back to Chelsea, he felt he could visit his sister without undue suspicion. Anyway, so he believed, and Major Slavering would be snoring.

But Major Slavering was not snoring. In fact, dressed for anonymity in a buckskin coat and without a hat, he was trotting not far behind his captain, for he had determined not to let Hew out of his sight until Alice and the head were apprehended. Neither Alice nor Dan noticed the figure that appeared and disappeared in Hew's wake. They were too busy keeping up and keeping out of sight themselves.

As soon as Hew reached the Cantankerings' house, he dismounted and pulled the large bell, tapping his foot impatiently until Mabel came to join him. At once, he slipped his arm around her and drew her close as they promenaded across the grass.

Mabel was in a mood. She had arrived at six A.M., as bidden by the duchess, so that she could organize the loading of the children's school books into the traveling cart. Although this meant rising at four, Mabel did not mind, but ever since she had set foot in the house, Lord Trotting had followed her about like a lovesick puppy, too shy to speak the words of love pulsing through his heart, but unable to leave her alone. What was worse, Lord Trotting's sisters and Mabel's charges, Lady Alicia Walker and Lady Araminta Walker, being young and wicked, had imitated their brother's sighs and found it highly amusing to recite, at full volume, the drippiest poetry they could find.

It was with relief that Mabel had made her excuses when the maid called up that her brother was downstairs. "Now," she said when they were out of earshot, "what are you doing here?"

As she knew he would, Hew rose at once to the bait. "Don't be an ass, Mabel. You know just why I have come."

Seeing real anxiety in Hew's eyes, Mabel relented, but only a little. "Mother nearly died of shock when she saw that head. Honestly, Hew, you could have killed her. And in case you're wondering, we hid it under my skirts."

"Under your skirts?" Hew sounded faintly shocked.

"Lord help us! Don't be such an old nanny. The man was dead! Did you not notice that I never stood up?" Hew looked stricken. "The danger—"

Mabel pinched his arm to hurt him. "A bit late to think of that." Her voice was sour. "Mother said you got carried away by some girl. Who on earth is she?"

"She's called Alice Towneley and she helped me climb off Temple Bar. I was stuck—well, you know how I am with heights. Anyway, that's not important. Where's the head now?"

Mabel looked sideways at her brother. "It's in a hatbox," she said. "I'm by way of taking it to Cantankering, from where, if you like, you can collect it and give it back to this ridiculous Alice whoever-she-is."

"Towneley," said Hew automatically.

"Well then," said Mabel. "Look. They're bringing the boxes out now. The head is in the painted one Lord Trotting gave me last Christmas, the one with hideous flowers and pudgy cherubs. It is wearing one of my hats. I think it looks rather fetching."

"How can you joke about this?" Hew sometimes itched to slap his sister.

Mabel made a face at him and they walked back to the house.

Alice, who had not been able to take her eyes off the two of them since Hew folded Mabel into the crook of his arm, now watched this unknown woman lean against him, clearly confiding some intimate secret or other. She felt as though somebody had punched her. Hew already had a sweetheart. Who else but a sweetheart would be drawn so close? All her stupid daydreams had been just that. She slumped a little in her saddle. She had been duped. No. She had duped herself. Hew had just been doing what he saw as his duty, helping her with Uncle Frank because she had helped him get down off Temple Bar. A tear scalded her cheek. She could not tell if it was from humiliation or disappointment, but whichever it was, it was horrid.

Dan had a somewhat different reaction. At first, he wanted to crow, but his initial surge of satisfaction at the sight of Hew's affections so evidently bestowed elsewhere quickly evaporated when he saw Alice's face. *For all her bravado, she's just a little girl*, he thought to himself. *Girls dream, especially of raven-haired captains in uniform. It's natural.* As he saw Alice's tear drop off her chin, a vision of his wife inconveniently popped up. He supposed that even she had once dreamed and briefly wondered what she would be dreaming now. *About my head in a wig bag*, he thought with a pang, and scratched his stubbled chin. He did not know what to say to Alice, so said nothing for the time being.

Major Slavering, who had hidden himself and his horse behind a large chestnut tree, watched Mabel show the coachman what were obviously her personal belongings in the luggage now piled on the pavement: one paltry trunk and a hatbox. Mabel was indicating that these should go with the baggage belonging to the servants. There was no wig bag, but, thought the major, wig bags were small things. Maybe he was too far away. Leaving the cover of the tree, he worked his way swiftly around the side streets behind the square until he reached the corner nearest the Cantankering house. It was almost inevitable that for his final approach he chose the very street on which Dan and Alice were lurking. The major at once saw the horses' rumps and was surprised to find two of his own men already stationed just where he wanted to be himself. He looked a little harder, wondering why the stumpy tail of one of the horses was so familiar.

Dan heard the hoofbeats and, at the same time, felt Belter's flanks begin to quiver. He turned. "It's the major," he hissed at Alice. "He's not in uniform but he must have followed Captain Ffrench too. He's heading straight for us. What shall we do?"

"Oh, God in Heaven!" Alice spluttered, wiping her nose on her glove. "I suppose we'd better ride into the square and around to the right, away from Captain Ffrench. Of course you were right, Dan Skinslicer," she added, furiously wiping her eyes as they moved off, "I think Captain Ffrench must have rescued the head and then—well, and then given it to his lady friend to keep." There was a sharp pause. "I hope she enjoyed it."

Dan didn't care about that now. Because he was nervous, he was holding Belter's reins too tight and the horse, fighting for more freedom, yanked at his bit and began to rock and buck, kicking his heels high in the air. Once he got started, he didn't want to stop. "Oh, glory!" Dan had not meant to shout at all, and certainly not to shout so loud, but the bucks were becoming so huge that he felt at any moment he would fly off. Alice leaned over, trying to help, but it was hopeless. The horse bucketed about and Dan yowled as he crashed like a lead weight on to the saddle's high pommel. At once the eyes of Major Slavering, Hew, and Mabel swiveled over and there was nothing Alice or Dan could do about it.

"Why!" Mabel exclaimed loudly and without thinking as she glanced at Alice's horse. "Isn't that Marron?"

At this, the rumble that had been gathering force at the bottom of Major Slavering's lungs erupted and his bellow made the windows shake. "Arrest them all! Arrest them all!" His face was puce as he leaped from the shadows. Gesticulating wildly with one hand at Dan and Alice and waving his reins with the other at Hew and Mabel, he set his horse this way and that, in agonies of indecision about which of the four to seize himself. Begging passersby to help him, he demanded, in the king's name, the arrest of all of them. "They are either impostors or traitors or both! Grab them! Nab them!" he cried. "Never mind the uniforms! Never mind anything! They are confounded enemies of King George II. They have even stolen a traitor's head. I order you again, grab them! Nab them!"

At the major's noisy hysteria, the local populace began to converge on the square. At first they shuffled about, unsure whether the bellower on his black horse was a madman who should be arrested himself or whether they should follow his order. But when Dan and Alice did not stop, they grew more excited and began to run.

Some grabbed Hew; others joined hands to

prevent Dan and Alice from breaking away. Kicking Marron hard, Alice shouted to Dan to mow them down, but Belter, ignoring Dan's every command, would not even attempt to charge forward and instead reversed at high speed until he brought his rider right within Major Slavering's grasp. Delighted, Slavering seized Dan and tried to wrestle him to the ground. Dan fought back with the rules of the gutter. It was a vicious match and the crowd was thrilled. This was terrific sport! They whooped and cheered, quickly taking sides.

It took Alice some moments to realize that Dan was not with her, but when she did, she pulled Marron around and drove him straight back, hoping to bulldoze Belter right past the major and sweep on through until she and Dan could together scatter the mass of unfriendly faces now surging around Hew. But everything got confused and, instead of finding herself where she wanted to be, Alice was soon wedged up against one of the luggage carts, struggling to keep her own seat as dozens of hands pulled and tugged at any part of her they could reach. Biting, kicking, and scratching as she was hooked and pummeled, Alice fought like a tiger, knowing for certain that if she was pulled out of the saddle, she would be lynched. She could hear somebody howling but never realized that it was herself.

Squashed almost underneath Marron was Mabel. But even had she been inclined to, she could not help Alice, for she was grappling with a curly-headed robber hell-bent on stealing the Cantankering luggage, beginning with the hatbox.

The weight of people was enormous and Marron, hardly able to keep his feet, was slowly pushed toward Hew. But it was Mabel Alice could hear. "The hatbox! Get the hatbox!" she was yelling, hanging on to the robber by his hair. The hatbox! Adrenalin pumped through Alice's veins. Uncle Frank! Twisting and shoving, she tried desperately to reach down, but failed. It was Hew, unable to draw his sword because of the crush, who eventually managed to pin the robber to the ground. A free-for-all followed, to which shrieks and groans provided a hideous accompaniment, and under this seething human soup both Hew and the hatbox were gradually submerged. Alice, spitting like a wildcat, dug her spurs as hard as she could into Marron's flanks and the horse struck out, his nostrils flaring and froth foaming from his mouth. At last Alice could see Hew bent double, determined to hang on to the hatbox despite being hammered on all sides. But it was a losing battle. When a huge man picked Hew up like a rat and shook him, determination was no longer enough. Hew could do nothing but let go and hear the bray of victory as the hatbox was lifted high in the air.

Alice, however, was ready. Quick as a flash, from her greater height, she seized the box's travel binding and the man suddenly found himself empty-handed. The weight nearly had Alice off, but Marron, maddened by both her spurs and the jabbing fingers of the crowd, reared up and jolted her back into the saddle. At once she slipped the binding loop over the cantle and tried to stop the box from swinging about and catching on the hilt of the sword that, because she had never worn one before, Alice had clean forgotten she was carrying. Her heart began to race even faster as with more enthusiasm than skill she tugged at the scabbard. Thirty-six inches of straight steel gleamed and flashed as she swept it before her, narrowly missing Marron's ears. The crowd drew back and Hew's bloodied face was briefly visible once more. "Hew, Hew!" Alice cried out to him, holding out her free hand. "Jump up here. Jump up. We can go off together."

Her face was so eager and fear had made her eyes brighter than ever. Hew raised his hand to her. But he knew his duty. He had seen what Alice had not. Dan and Major Slavering were no longer wrestling. Slavering had been pitched off his horse. But while in his victory Dan, like Alice, had drawn his sword and was almost free of the crowd, Slavering had captured the most powerful weapon of all. He had Mabel and was pulling her onto the luggage wagon. Hew could not leave her and Slavering knew it.

When Alice realized the reason for Hew's hesitation, her eyes grew dark and unfriendly. She called out to Hew again. He heard her only too clearly and longed, with all his heart, to answer her call. What did it matter that he hardly knew her or that she was too grand for him? It was enough to know with thundering certainty that he wanted to be with her. She seemed so hopeful and strong, the kind of girl who could clear your head and make you feel brilliantly alive. He wanted so badly to tell her this, to throw his heart at her feet. But he stopped his ears against her. This was not the time. He could not abandon Mabel. The crowd closed in on him again.

Dan had no qualms about either Hew or Mabel. His only concern was Alice. Brandishing his sword like a cudgel, he roared defiance, booted Belter into a canter, and, as he passed Marron, slapped the horse's rump with the blade's flat edge. Marron lurched forward, flipping the reins out of Alice's hands and neatly into Dan's. Dan did not let go. Pulling Marron behind him, with Alice sobbing in girlish indignation and frustration every step of the way, Dan bludgeoned a passage through the riot and set off across the grass to make good their escape. Alice might drum her heels against Marron's sides and the horse might buck and plunge, but Dan kept going forward. Cursing and swearing in a way Dan hated, Alice twisted backward. She saw Hew clamber up onto the wagon. She saw Major Slavering let go of his hostage. She saw a blade flash high above Hew's head.

Hours later, ringing through her whole body, she could still hear Mabel's scream.

Nobody was allowed to visit Hew in the barracks prison except, for the first two days, his mother and Mabel, and Hew was glad when their visits were discontinued. Mrs. Ffrench was never less than dignified but the pain in her face haunted him.

Apart from many bruises, Hew had emerged relatively unscathed from both the mob and Major Slavering. The hovering blade that caused Mabel to scream had not been used to injure him. Major Slavering wanted Hew a prisoner, not a dead man. Prisoners were far more fun. Yet although his cell was ankle-deep in slime and rat droppings and the image of his head on a pike was enough to make his raven locks lose their luster, Hew had no regrets. For a start, surely, now that he had Hew, Major Slavering would give up pursuing Alice. It should be enough sport to vent his venom on a soldier he had always despised. And in spite of the stories the major and others would inevitably love to spread about, branding Hew a traitor,

Hew also knew in his heart that his honor was unstained. He had helped Alice because she was just a girl trying to do the best by her uncle. Sometimes, during the wretched nights, when the dark was absolute and men went mad, Hew asked himself if he would have done the same had Alice been old and warty. He hoped the answer was yes, but he could not deny that those cornflower eyes and the stubborn set of Alice's mouth had made his duty much sweeter. Yet it must surely count for something that he had given up the escape Alice offered in order to protect Mabel, even though Mabel had been singularly ungrateful.

Major Slavering also lay awake thinking, but the tenor of his dreams was rather different. What he wanted from Hew was nothing short of a full, execution-worthy confession. In effect, Hew must declare that, since the battle of Culloden, he had changed sides and was now sympathetic to Bonnie Prince Charlie's cause. This would give the king no option but to sanction Hew's hanging, drawing, and quartering, and this was what Major Slavering now desired above all things. That captain had ideas above his station. He should, literally, be cut down to size.

However, as Hew was unlikely to declare himself a traitor of his own accord, Slavering decided to persuade him. If Hew agreed to condemn himself, the major was prepared to forget about dragging Alice and

Dan back to London to face trial and he would forget about Colonel Towneley's head too, just for good measure. So long as Alice and Dan never returned to London and they buried the head somewhere where nobody would ever be tempted to dig it up, they would be left alone.

When Slavering finally visited Hew, he outlined his plan in terms both clipped and clear. Hew stood in silence until the major grew impatient. "Well, Captain F-f-f-french? Where's your gallantry now? Too cowardly to save your ladylove, eh?"

But Hew would not reply and eventually Slavering gave up and went away.

That night Hew lay in an agony of indecision. To save Alice he would do anything. But if he confessed to treachery, his mother would suffer and suffer grievously. Nobody would want to associate with her, or want their servants to be seen dropping off the sewing on which her income depended. And then there was Mabel. Lord Trotting could not possibly marry the sister of an executed traitor. How could Hew conspire to ruin his whole family? He would be worse than his father. He could not do it, not even if Alice herself asked him.

When Slavering visited the next morning, Hew greeted him again with silence, and the following morning after that. But Slavering was determined to break him and made sure that his former captain starved and suffered. On some days, Hew was left alone with the rats. Those were good days. On other days, Slavering would send the prison guards to talk to him. Those were bad days. On other days still, Major Slavering himself would pay a visit. Those were worse.

With troopers scouring the country for them, Alice and Dan made their way stealthily northward, discarding their dragoons' uniforms and keeping only their swords and horses. The turnpike roads were full of tramping soldiers, so the two fugitives were forced onto disused tracks thick with summer growth. It rained torrentially and the miles seemed very long. Even the horses grew dispirited.

Dan tried everything he could to coax Alice to talk to him, but she sat on Marron, hunched and silent, as she was led away from danger and toward home. Every morning Dan told her that she would soon see her mother and father again, but every evening she had only one question. What right had she to make a good man like Hew destroy himself to protect the head of somebody he neither knew nor cared about, particularly when that somebody was already dead. "Hew's ladylove, or wife, or whatever she was," she added, trying to sound matter-of-fact, "will be right never to forgive me." She went on and on, always ending plaintively that she could not rest because she didn't even know if Hew was dead or alive.

Every evening, with Job-like patience, Dan listened to the familiar litany and was ready with his answer. "Captain Ffrench didn't do what he did for the dead but for the living. He wants you to be able to bury your uncle Frank's head because that's what you want to do. Now, missy, you must pull yourself together. That's what the poor man would want."

"He did it because he felt sorry for me." Even in her distress, Alice was never short of a reply. "Or maybe that girl told him to."

After a while, Dan tried a different tack, reassuring Alice that if Hew was still alive, he would be tried, probably not executed but only sent to the galleys. He was a hero of Culloden after all. Alice seemed almost more horrified by this and reminded Dan of his own terror of the sea. "Ah," said Dan philosophically, "but Captain Ffrench won't ever have smelled a dead cabin boy, so he won't know how bad it is, will he?"

It was unsurprising that Alice found none of this comforting, particularly with the rain seeping down her collar, and Dan soon gave up his initial hope that she was too sensible, or perhaps too heartless, to pine after Hew for long. Alice never asked how he himself was doing and eventually Dan just concentrated on traveling. He had tried his best.

★

After ten days or so, however, Alice shook him awake, declaring that she wanted to find "that girl who kindly put Uncle Frank into this hatbox." Her fingers plucked at his shirt. She wanted to go right now. She could not like the girl, but she wanted to see her anyway. There might be news of Hew.

Dan pulled himself up. The ants had been at him and, as he picked them out of his ears, he saw that although Alice's face was filthy and pinched, her chin had regained some of its stubbornness and she had already heaved the saddles onto the backs of the horses. "That's madness," he told her, but his heart was lighter as she ate some of the bread he had stolen the day before. "She probably lives in London and we can hardly go back there, missy. Even you must see that."

"Well," said Alice, stamping her foot, "maybe we don't have to go to London. The lady looked as if she was going on a journey. If we knew who she was, perhaps we could find out where she's gone."

Dan shrugged. Who was going to tell them? The birds?

Alice chewed harder on the bread, then suddenly hurled it away. "The hatbox," she said, and color began to flow back into her cheeks. "The hatbox Uncle Frank's head is in is hers, Dan. Maybe there is a clue in there."

"You're not going to disturb the poor colonel again?" Dan was horrified. "He must feel like a regular parcel. Can't he just sit tight until it's time to bury him?"

But Alice wasn't listening. She ran to Marron, pulled the hatbox off his saddle, and tugged it open.

Uncle Frank was almost hidden under Mabel's bonnet, a broad affair, generally colored pale lilac and elaborately decorated. The feathers that were glued around the brim drooped over the colonel's nose and stuck to his tar-blackened straggles. Had Frank been alive, the effect would have been undignified. Now that he was dead, it was preposterous and his expression was more than unhappy. Alice apologized as she set him gently on the grass.

Dan stared. "Oh, the poor man," he said with feeling, and wiped away the fluff that had accumulated on Uncle Frank's forehead. The colonel needed a shave, so Dan noticed, for hair still grows after death, but even Dan could not bring himself to use his own razor. It was Dan who found what Alice was looking for. "There," he said, pointing to a small inscription on the inside of the hatbox lid, which Alice, in her haste, had pushed to one side. "There."

"What does it say?"

Dan shifted. "You read it."

Alice looked at him curiously and leaned over. "Mabel Ffrench," she read aloud, "care of the Duke of Cantankering, Cantankering Castle, Cantankering, Cantankeringshire." She sank back on her heels. "Mabel Ffrench. Miss Mabel Ffrench. *Miss* Mabel *Ffrench*. Oh, Dan Skinslicer! The lady is not Hew's ladylove, nor even his wife. She's his *sister*! Well I never. Hew's *sister*." As she said the words over and over, the haunted look that so upset Dan vanished. "Hew's sister. The girl's his sister." She jumped up. "Come on, Dan Skinslicer, we must go to her." She gave a skip. "And to think . . . And I thought . . ."

"You thought too quickly," said Dan, a trifle glumly.

"I suppose I did," Alice agreed, "but don't be such a grump, Dan. Maybe Hew is still alive. Maybe he is. Wouldn't that be marvelous!" She did not look at Dan again, but hurried to put Uncle Frank back in the hatbox. She barely noticed at first that the head was now looking at her with a kind of disappointed sorrow and, when she did notice, she chose to put her uncle's expression down to the ugliness of the hat he had been obliged to wear. "Sorry," she whispered, "we'll get that silly hat off of you as soon as possible, but just now it is such a good disguise. I hope you understand." Dan had to help her get the lid on and Alice was disconcerted to notice that when Dan's hands appeared, Uncle Frank's expression changed to one of sympathy. It brought her up short and she looked at Dan properly for the first time in days. Her heart smote her. "How is your shoulder now?" she asked. "It seems ages since I dressed it."

Dan made the hatbox secure. "It's all right, missy," he said shortly as he tightened Belter's girth. "You can check it tonight. Look." He gestured to the sky. The sun was breaking through and, after the chill, the wind was breathing warm through the bracken. "If we're to find this Cantankering Castle, we'd best get going."

Alice didn't argue. The hatbox, soaked once too often, was beginning to crumble, but she didn't care as it squashed against her knee. Even the horses sensed a new purpose and trotted willingly through the drying mud. Alice got directions from a tinker and sped on, but Dan, although happy to see her so lively again even if the reason gave him an odd pang in his heart, had many misgivings as he followed behind. He had no idea what they might find at Cantankering Castle and did not share Alice's evidently unshakeable belief that their welcome would be friendly.

When they had been going about an hour, he was glad that Marron slackened the pace until he realized that Alice was calling to him to read a signpost she had missed.

"I can't!" Dan called back. "My eyesight's too poor."

"Nonsense!" Alice shouted. "You could see enough to catch me off Temple Bar."

He insisted and Alice turned back to read the

signpost for herself. They rode on, but after a few minutes Alice turned to him and said in what she considered to be her nicest voice, "The truth is that you can't read, can you, Dan Skinslicer? I thought you couldn't when we opened the hatbox so I missed the signpost on purpose. I could easily teach you, you know," she continued tactlessly. "You have done so much for me, maybe I could do this for you?"

At this, Dan fell into a sulk. Who on earth did Alice think she was? He left her question hanging in the air and, when he did reply, it was in peevish tones. "I didn't grow up in your fancy home, lounging around with books," he said. "I went to work when I was five. I don't expect you will go to work at all." He kicked Belter unnecessarily hard and overtook Marron. "And anyway," he shouted over his shoulder, "I can read some things. I can read the Bible and I found the address in the hatbox."

"You can only read the Bible because the stories are so familiar," replied Alice, riled. "It's easy to read words you already know. And what's the use in finding a label if you can't tell what it says?"

Dan was suddenly more depressed than irritated. What was he doing here, playing nursemaid to this unconscionable girl? She could speak in a nice voice but she was not a nice person, for she led him on, then knocked him back, always sighing after a handsome captain and taking a toiling hangman utterly for granted. *I had a wife and a job before I met her,* he thought. Now he had nothing except a black horse that didn't belong to him. He had even lost all the tools of his trade. He tried to remember when he had last seen them but couldn't.

They rode in silence. Alice purposefully pushed past him and Dan let her. It was another hour before she turned around to make sure he was still there. Then it was clear at once, from Dan's slumped shoulders, what she had done. At first she was cross. However, after a while, she was sorry and eased Marron back until they rode stirrup to stirrup. Dan would not look at her, but Alice stayed beside him and after a while, when the road grew smooth, she took off her hat and shook out her hair. "Race you?" she offered.

In the bright sun, even in his mood, Dan noticed that, despite the easiness of her tone, Alice was anxious. His heart softened, then he groaned inside himself. Try as he might to build defenses against her, she had only to look a certain way and he melted like butter. He told himself strictly not to, but what was the use? He slapped Belter with the flat of his hand and his broad face cleared again. "I'll beat you to the next milepost, whether I can read it or not. Now, take care of the colonel's head. That's your handicap." As they galloped, neck to neck, he felt his spirits lift. Alice, grateful and happy that Dan had forgiven her so easily, allowed him to win.

Once in Cantankeringshire, it was not difficult to find Cantankering, a large market town, over which Cantankering Castle loomed. The sight of it, half beneficent protector, half threatening bully, gave Dan the jitters but Alice would not be dissuaded. "I've got to go in," she told him as he let Belter dawdle. "I won't leave until I know Hew's fate. But maybe it is best if I go on my own. I'll go on foot and say I'm a friend of Mabel's."

"For goodness' sake, missy, be careful," Dan begged. "She may not want to see you."

Alice just gave him a look.

The road was getting busier and although a shabbily dressed couple were nothing special, even if the girl was riding astride, people did look curiously at the identical bobtailed horses. Neither as neat nor as glossy as they had been when Alice and Dan commandeered them, their military gait and bearing had, nevertheless, still not deserted them.

The castle portcullis was raised and the gates were open. Delighted at this good portent, Alice dismounted neatly. "I'll go in now. Look! I don't even have to knock," she said.

However, the gate was swinging wide not to let

visitors in but to let a group of people out. A dozen or so Kingston's dragoons were headed straight toward them. Dan made a grab for Alice and swung her back into the saddle as they at once plunged away, back into the crowd they had just left.

They were too late. The sharp-eyed captain—Hew's replacement—let out a cry. "Look! Look, men! There they are! On, men, on and get 'em!" There was a general spurring of horses and many great whoops as the troopers, sick to the teeth of their hitherto fruitless searching, determined that they were not going to be denied their prey now.

It was an uneven chase. Alice did not even have time to get her feet into her stirrups and Marron and Belter, homesick for their fellows, fled only with reluctance. "Come on, come on," urged Dan, in panic. They crashed through a dogfight taking place in the middle of the road, knocking spectators into the dust as they skimmed over the shafts of the carriages and carts used to mark out the makeshift ring. Dan found himself safely on the other side, but Alice was not so lucky. One of the dogs, already maddened with pain, forgot its rival and launched itself at Marron instead. It missed the horse but clamped its jaws gamely on Alice's skirts and she was suddenly involved in a tug-of-war she could not win. *Oh, why did your skirt never rip when you wanted it to?* All too soon she found herself sliding closer and closer toward the ground and eventually fell off.

At once Dan yanked his reins and charged back, just managing to sweep Alice up in front of him on Belter. Marron, now confused, followed on as Dan tried again to make good their escape. Draped over the front of Belter's saddle, Alice was jolted and jarred, but Dan's strong hand kept her safely wedged and, once through the straggling ends of the town, the going was easier, with fewer people and conveyances blocking the way. Yet the cobblestones were cruel on galloping legs and Belter was not at all keen on the breakneck speed Dan wanted from him. Marron trailed behind, looking half back, half forward, with Uncle Frank's hatbox still swinging at his shoulder.

"We must catch Marron, Dan Skinslicer, we must catch Marron. We can't lose Uncle Frank again!" Alice hiccupped.

Dan nodded—it was no time to argue—and leaned back to encourage the horse to come alongside. Marron sped up, but his bridle was always just out of reach. They galloped out of the town and made for the woods, plowing straight through a flock of sheep. Belter found the turf here more to his liking, but with no rider to push him and the grass so tempting, Marron began to dawdle. Alice implored him to hurry, holding out her hand as if it was full of sweetmeats, but he took no notice and, in the end, Dan had to pull Belter up and wait. It was clear that if they wanted to keep Uncle Frank, Alice must remount Marron and ride him to safety.

It was dreadful watching the troopers storming toward them, but at last Marron came near enough for Dan to take one last chance. Straining every muscle, he stretched and hovered, then caught the elusive straps. Alice sobbed with relief. She had no time to swap horses, so she just yelled at Marron as loudly as she could, making both horses canter with more enthusiasm toward a dense clump of trees. As soon as they reached them, Alice tumbled to the ground and clambered into her own saddle.

It was too late to move now. The dragoons were already crashing through the thicket behind them, fanning out, trying to find which way their quarry had gone. They missed seeing the path Dan had taken, so, very slowly and in perfect unison, Dan and Alice slipped deeper beneath the shadowed canopy of a huge oak. With black horses they might yet escape detection. All would be well, provided they were quiet as mice.

It was then that Marron, spying an equine friend, neighed a loud and cheerful greeting.

11

The dragoons quickly surrounded them. Dan tried to barge a way through for Alice, urging her to flee as he took the blows and parried the sword thrusts, but despite his best efforts they were both taken, their hands bound behind their backs and their feet tied together under the horses' bellies. They were whisked straight to Cantankering Castle, where the duke, much surprised, found himself obliged to provide a cart to transport the prisoners and Uncle Frank's head back to London. The clattering and fuss in the courtyard was loud enough to carry to the schoolroom and Hew's sister and her two charges came running down to see what was going on. Mabel stared when she saw Alice, recognizing her at once from the riot in Lincoln's Inn Fields. Her stare was not friendly and Alice had very quickly to give up any notion that Mabel would happily share news of Hew, or indeed address a word to her at all. Alice climbed into the cart with dread in her heart.

"Don't say 'I told you so,'" she whispered to Dan.

"I'm saying nothing at all," he muttered back.

Their return to London was mercifully quick, for the dragoons headed straight down the turnpike, making a travesty of the weary meanderings Dan and Alice had endured in order to keep out of sight. The two of them sat close together, with Uncle Frank beside them, glad that their conveyance was a closed one so that they were at least spared the indignity of having things thrown at them in the villages through which they passed. At regular intervals they stopped at coaching inns and the troopers ordered changes of cart horse "in the king's name." *If only I could meet the beastly king,* Alice thought, holding on to Dan for comfort, *I am sure I could show him that we meant no harm.* When she confided these thoughts to Dan, he humored her but he could already feel the chilly tickle of the hangman's noose.

Once they were back in London, Major Slavering couldn't contain himself and had Hew dragged out immediately to witness their disheveled disgrace. "Well, Captain F-f-f-french," he gloated, "I wonder if this tasty girl knows that she has you to thank for her less-than-comfortable quarters?"

Hew, blinking in the unaccustomed light, pulled himself up from the floor. It was not possible for his complexion to be any paler, but when he saw Alice he could have passed for a ghost. At the same time Alice, when she saw the emaciated and bedraggled state Hew was in, lost any delight in knowing for certain that he was still alive.

Slavering found this spectacle very satisfactory. "Did you know, Mistress Alice Towneley," he said, deliberately conversational, "that Captain Ffrench could have saved you all this nonsense? He had it within his power to make sure I forgot all about you. All he had to do was reveal to the world that he is not really a supporter of King George, but secretly supports that overdressed Jacobite impostor, just like your traitorous Uncle Frank. But he was too cowardly, poor old Captain Two-Effs, so here we all are. Now, I know what to do with him, but the question is, what are we to do with you?"

"Touch her, Slavering, and you'll hang yourself," Hew croaked.

"Oh, I'll not hang," smiled the major, pushing Hew into a chair. "On the contrary, the king rewards those who get heads returned to Temple Bar and we'll have this one"—he kicked the hatbox—"back up there before you know it." He walked over to Alice. "Now, my dear," he said, lifting up her chin with his thumb and enjoying the look in her eyes, "I'm going to ask Captain Ffrench once more, in your presence, if he will save you by telling us the truth about himself. Come, come." He let go of Alice's chin and pulled her chair around so that she and Hew were facing each other. Dan, objecting loudly, was pushed into the corner.

Slavering sat himself down behind a desk, for all the world like a notary settling a dispute between neighbors over a hedge. "Captain Ffrench," he began without further ado, "will you confess to harboring sympathy for the cause of Charles Edward Stuart, known as Bonnie Prince Charlie, against our lawful monarch, George II?" The major suddenly saw a joke. "You could just say 'I will,' as if you were getting married!"

Hew turned to face his tormentor. "Why all this trumpery playacting, Major?" he asked. "We fought together at Culloden and we fought well. Why are you going to have me executed?"

The major leaned back. "Because you defied me, Captain Ffrench," he said with chilling simplicity, "but mainly because I can." He tapped his fingers on the desk. "I wonder . . ."—he glanced down to see where his kick had sent the hatbox—"should we get Colonel Towneley out to see what he can add to our discussions?"

Alice shrank away as Slavering retrieved the hatbox and opened it. But even he hesitated when he saw

Uncle Frank's head under Mabel's hat. He turned on Dan. "You! Skinslicer! Come and deal with the traitor's head," he ordered brusquely. "You are used to having blood on your hands. Come on, man, look sharp."

With a helpless look at Alice, Dan shuffled over. Taking care first to remove the hat, he carefully eased Uncle Frank out and settled him on the desk amid the hanks of wigmaker's horsehair. The dead face was a strange and not very attractive color, but the countenance was far from repulsive and Dan found himself muttering apologies for this new disturbance. The colonel's eyes seemed not only to forgive but to offer warm encouragement.

This was Major Slavering's first close-quarters encounter with a disembodied head and it took him some time to approach it face-to-face, as it were. And certainly there was no warm encouragement for *him* in the colonel's eyes. Indeed, Frank offered only a scowl that, for some reason, made Slavering feel as though he had eaten a hedgehog. "Well," he choked, trying to look at Alice but unable to drag his gaze from Uncle Frank, "what a sight! I have to say, Mistress Towneley, at least your head will be a great deal prettier."

Alice couldn't help giving a small squeak.

Hew leaped up. "You know that the king would never sanction the execution of a girl like Alice," he declared loudly.

Slavering swung around. With the head behind him, he was back to his usual vile self. "I know nothing of the sort. Rather the opposite. Head stealing, horse stealing, treason, and treachery"—he counted Alice's offenses off on his fingers—"she will need a good advocate. The king shows no mercy to traitors and criminals of whatever age or sex."

"I have my horse back and so do you." Hew refused to be quiet.

"I doubt whether Justice Peckersmith will grant her pardon on that basis." Major Slavering laughed mirthlessly. "But then she could be spared any kind of trial at all if only you will confess your own crimes. All depends on you, Captain Ffrench. As I have said before, just a couple of the right words and we could lose her and her uncle Frank on the road north. Perhaps it might help to ask yourself this: should a captain in Kingston's Light Horse be too lily-livered to die to give a young girl back her freedom?" He walked over to Alice, drew his sword, and delicately traced around her neck with the point. She tried not to waver, but was not very successful. "An easy chop for the executioner, this neck, wouldn't you say, Skinslicer?"

Dan was on his knees. "Look, Major Slavering—sir— your majorness, your honorableness. Why not just execute me? I'm the guilty one really. After all, it was me who persuaded missy here to get away with the head. I could've brought the colonel back, I really could've. But I didn't. And I'll say whatever you like. I'll make green blue or say fish fly. Do you hear? Whatever you like, so then you can string me up and spike my head. But, sir, your most eminent sirness, let her go. Please let her go. I'm ready for a public confession. Just tell me what to say and I'll say it, or get somebody to write it down and I'll put my thumbprint on it."

Slavering snorted but Alice almost cried, so stirred was she by Dan's heroism. He would sacrifice himself for her! She didn't deserve it. Yet his courage gave her courage of her own. "You will not, Dan Skinslicer," she stated. "None of this is your fault, so please get up and let's have no more talk of confessions and thumbprints." She pulled at Major Slavering's arm. "You know full well that the whole responsibility for Uncle Frank's head and the stolen horses lies with me and, although I may not be as brave as my uncle Frank, I'll never be sorry for what I did. Do your worst, Major Slavering, but leave Dan alone. He's perfectly innocent. If I have to die, I'm quite ready." She hoped very much that this was true.

Hew exclaimed, but Alice raised her hand as imperiously as she could. "As for Captain Ffrench," she said, "he is as good a servant of King George the— well, whatever number George we have reached—as you are. It's too stupid to pretend he's not. So I don't know what you really want, Major Slavering. All I know is that you're not going to get it."

At this, Hew reached over to Alice and the next thing Slavering saw was their fingers slip together. Then his wrath was mighty. Uttering the foulest oaths, he raised his sword and brought it slicing down between them, almost burning their skin as their hands parted just in time and the sword clanged to the floor. "You'll all go to trial, then," he exploded. "All of you. There will be no more offers of ways out. Not one of you will be spared." He roared for soldiers to come and remove the prisoners, slamming the flat of his hand again and again on the table. How had this silly child managed to inject the soul of that two-effed ninny with iron? He stopped raging long enough to scrutinize Alice as she went past. She stared right back at him and her stare, disconcertingly, reminded him of Uncle Frank's. Yet had he turned to look at the colonel's head at this particular moment, he might have been surprised, for as Hew, Dan, and Alice were hustled through the door, Uncle Frank's expression was no longer either encouraging or scowling. In fact, he was, quite openly, beaming with pride. Nor did this beam diminish when the troopers drew lots to see who would dare put him back in his hatbox. Nor even when he was dropped unceremoniously inside and the lid clapped on again.

It was still there when the troopers kicked the box around just to show they cared nothing for heads. And when finally the box was hurled into the cell along with Alice, Dan, and Hew to await the judgment of Lord Chief Justice Peckersmith, Uncle Frank was beaming still.

The trial gained notoriety before it had even begun. The combination of a dashing Kingston's Light Horse captain, a girl, a hangman, and a head was irresistible to the newspapers springing up in London and the news traveled north. The *Manchester Gazette* and the *Newcastle Courant* carried reports and people heard rumors of it in taverns and coaching houses from the Welsh valleys to the Suffolk fishing harbors and from London to Berwick. The more interest it aroused, the more dashing, beautiful, and noble, or disgraceful, brazen, and wicked, depending on your point of view, Hew, Alice, and Dan became. Slavering's troopers found themselves in heavy demand to fill in details, which they did with more enthusiasm than accuracy, happily supping the free ale that was their reward. Whole families made outings to Temple Bar to look up at the empty spike on which, they were told, Uncle Frank's head would shortly be reinstated.

The news did not, however, permeate behind the hilly fastness that cut Towneley Hall off from the outside world. The Towneleys heard news only when it was at least two months out of date. So while his brother's dead head and his daughter's living body languished in a prison cell and were the subject of taproom gossip, Sir Thomas Towneley measured his raindrops and his wife busied herself turning her cheeses and telling her rosary beads. When they thought of Alice at all, it was with regretful sighs that her nurse had not instilled in her the habit of weekly letter writing.

Lady Widdrington and Ursula, on the other hand, knew about Alice's capture almost at once. Bunion heard the news first at the coachmaker's and, with one wheel only half-repaired, jumped onto the box and galloped back to Grosvenor Square to tell the footman, who ran upstairs to tell the two ladies, who were squabbling in the small drawing room, as they had been ever since Alice disappeared.

This morning, Ursula was, as usual, flapping her hands and hopping up and down, screeching, "For God's sake, how many times? Can't you understand? Frank was never coming to dinner. He has lost his head and Alice has gone off with it. LOST HIS HEAD, you daft old wig wearer. God give me strength! Do I have to spell it out again? Frank's dead and Alice is missing.

Now, for pity's sake, WHAT ARE WE GOING TO DO?"

Lady Widdrington's mouth contracted to a pinhead. "How foolish you look and what nonsense you talk, Ursula. Heads are not things you mislay. Although,"— her lips wrinkled ever more—"it might be better if you could mislay yours. If you found a different one, you might catch a husband yet."

Ursula's wig had just begun one of the more violent of its characteristic wobbles when the youngest footman exploded into the room, his excitement banishing any sense of propriety. Perched like a bird on her chair, Lady Widdrington listened, her head darting back and forth as he told his tale. Ursula squawked periodically. When the torrent of words came to an end, she was triumphant.

"There now, Mother, what did I tell you?" she gabbled, but faltered when she saw her mother's face.

Just for a moment Lady Widdrington was a trembling old lady, jolting with shock from her bald head to her wizened toes. "Ursula?" Her voice was quavery. "Ursula? Did he say that Frank is dead?"

"Yes, Mother."

"And Alice entirely at the cruel mercy of a skinslicer?"

The footman tried to put her right about this, but Ursula shut him up. Desperate to take full advantage of this one moment of lucidity, she was not going to waste it on a hangman. "Something like that, Mother. But lordy, lordy, who cares? We must run from Grosvenor Square before they come to arrest us too. Hurry, Mother, hurry, hurry, hurry. We'll set off at once for my Aunt Blackstone's house in Chiswick—BUNION! BUNION! FETCH THE CARRIAGE! Come ON, Mother."

Lady Widdrington stared at Ursula. "I don't like Chiswick." Tears bumped an uneven course down her cheeks.

"We can't stay here." Ursula shook her mother hard and tried a new tactic. "Listen, Mother. Frank wouldn't want us to be executed. Listen, listen! Can't you hear his voice? I do believe his ghost is telling us to go to Chiswick! Gooooo toooo Chiiiiiswiiiick. I can hear him, can't you?"

Lady Widdrington's eyes rolled and Ursula's heart sank. But suddenly her mother sprang up. "Send for Bunion," she cried rather unnecessarily. "The coach, the coach! Harness the horses!"

Babbling with relief, Ursula scrambled to her feet. "Didn't you hear? Bring the coach around! Bring it around at once! My mother demands it!"

Minutes later they bumped into each other at the front door. Ursula was wearing her traveling cloak, Lady Widdrington her most sparkling jewelry. "For goodness' sake, Mother," Ursula shrieked, "you won't need jewelry if you don't have a HEAD." She was cut off, midcry, by a knock on the door. With a strangled hiccup, she scurried into the shadows, her nose twitching like a terrified mouse. Surely they were not to be arrested now, just at this last moment?

Lady Widdrington stayed exactly where she was and settled her priceless tiara even more crookedly into her wig.

The tiara was the first thing that caught the eye of Mrs. Ffrench as the door was opened and it took her a little time to adjust her sights downward to the powdered face beneath. "Lady Widdrington?"

"Who else would I be?" Alice's grandmother fixed Mrs. Ffrench with a baleful glare.

Mrs. Ffrench tried to sound strong. "I'm Captain Hew Ffrench's mother."

"Who?"

Mrs. Ffrench explained, trying not to be disconcerted by Ursula, who had crept out of the shadows and was standing behind Lady Widdrington, signaling through bizarre gesticulations that her mother was, in fact, dotty. Lady Widdrington, who could see Ursula's pantomime reflected in the paint on the door, kicked smartly backward as she listened, catching her daughter's ankle with commendable accuracy.

None of this filled Mrs. Ffrench with hope. She had come to Grosvenor Square to beg Alice's grandmother to use any influence she had to prevent Hew from receiving the ultimate punishment. She herself was going to write to the Duke of Cantankering, she said, but she needed to know that Lady Widdrington would not try to gain her granddaughter's release at the expense of Hew's life. As for Dan Skinslicer, Mrs. Ffrench was worried about him too. The man had a wife, so everybody was saying, and it seemed he had been caught up in this escapade by mischance. "And so was my son," Mrs. Ffrench insisted firmly. "He was trying to help Alice get Colonel Towneley's head home out of the goodness of his heart."

Lady Widdrington tilted her own head farther and farther over as she listened until eventually her wig began to topple and plumped onto the floor, the tiara skidding under the sideboard. As Ursula scrabbled to rescue both from the dust, Mrs. Ffrench gave up entirely. These lunatic women, with their chalky scalps and eye-popping fashion sense, were from another planet entirely. She should never have come.

Reunited with her wig and tiara, Lady Widdrington pushed past Mrs. Ffrench, hopped quickly through the door, down the steps, and, before Ursula could stop her, sprang into the carriage that Bunion had obediently brought around. Fizzing like champagne, she implored him to whip up the horses and was gone. Ursula smacked her hands together. "Stop! Oh, stop! STOP! Don't you love me at all? Are you leaving me to the mercy of the mob, YOU UNFEELING CROW?"

Mrs. Ffrench watched, wanting to do some smacking herself. When Ursula ran back into the house in a fine fit of hysterics, Mrs. Ffrench did not stay to comfort her.

Lord Chief Justice Peckersniff was at home, a handkerchief over his nose. In either hand he held a beautifully heavy bag filled with money he wanted to invest. He did not wish to make a great fortune, only enough to buy a very large house in which he could have some hope of escaping from his wife, the very woman who had been having new teeth fitted on the day of Uncle Frank's execution. Despite all Peckersniff's hopes, the new teeth had done nothing to sweeten his wife's breath, which was still whiffy as a dead pig, and while the Lord Chief Justice did not wish to divorce her, he could no longer bear to be in the same room.

When he heard a carriage draw up, he stuffed the bags into the false seat of his chair and hid behind the curtains, only to find Lady Widdrington staring at him through the window. He could scarcely not ask her in. To start with, their conversation was extremely jerky, since Lady Widdrington could not quite remember why she had come and Peckersniff would not help her. Naturally, he knew now that the girl he had spotted on the gallows at Uncle Frank's execution was not the hangman's niece but the offspring of highly respectable parents and this rather less respectable grandparent. However, he most certainly didn't want to discuss Alice in case he was required to sit in judgment over her on the bench. "My dear lady, dear lady," he said gallantly after a few very uncomfortable minutes, "how well your wig looks, really very well, but my, my, is that the time? I must keep a very important appointment. Can I show you—"

"My granddaughter has a head," said Lady Widdrington. She had been rocking from foot to foot, but now she approached him very fast and Peckersniff had to swerve out of her way.

"And a very pretty one too, I expect," he replied nervously. He vaguely recalled that Alice *had* been pretty and anyway, in his experience, all grandchildren were pretty to their grandparents.

"She must keep it."

"Indeed she must," agreed the judge. "And I am sure, dear lady, that she will, sure she will, I say."

Lady Widdrington frowned. "And there's a man with two effs," she said, "although why he has two effs I couldn't say. Anyway, he should keep his, or it will end up in a hatbox, like Frank. Or is he coming to dinner?"

She looked expectantly at Peckersniff. "He's not, though, is he? Body in a box. Was that because Frank only has one eff?"

Peckersniff waved his hands, as if by catching the words and putting them in a different order he might discover what on earth they meant. Lady Widdrington followed his hands for a moment or two, then began to cry. Peckersniff was horrified. Now he would have to give her his handkerchief! He stood like a paralyzed heron, one bandy leg rooted to the floor. But it was no good. He couldn't allow a lady's nose to run uncovered. He leaned toward Lady Widdrington. Unfortunately, she mistook his gesture, ignored the handkerchief, and wiped powder all over his smoking jacket.

Some faint girlhood memory triggered by the feel of the silk lapel cheered Lady Widdrington. She stopped crying and swiftly became spookily flirtatious. "Oh, sir!" She gave a girlish simper. "I want my granddaughter back, and the hatbox she is so attached to, and the man with two effs, because his mother asks so nicely. You could do that for me, couldn't you?" She rolled back her lips. At least *her* gums weren't black. "I've a daughter," she wheedled. "She's a little plain but you'd never know it in the dark."

"Madam, madam, madam!" cried the scandalized judge. "Please. I have a wife, a wife, indeed, whom I'm expecting shortly, expecting shortly, d'ye hear? Now, I can do nothing to help you. Nothing. Justice must be done, justice I say. That is clear. That is sufficient. That is all." He remembered his position and frowned the frown of a man with the power of life or death. It had taken a long time to perfect this frown, but it had been more useful than a whole study of books. It was useful now. Lady Widdrington backed away and, skillful as a sheepdog, Lord Chief Justice Peckersniff hurried her out the way she had come in.

It was not until he saw her face peering from the carriage window, like a ferret in a hutch, that he sank into his chair and placed a clean handkerchief over his face. But there was still no peace. Under his left buttock was something hard and bulgy. He tugged it out. It was a jeweled bracelet, thick as a horse's girth, and valuable as a king's ransom. The scrawly writing on the note attached simply said, "Ffor you iff you ffree Alice, Ffrank, and Ffrench." Peckersniff held the treasure out as if it was contaminated, but the diamonds and rubies winked their devilish eyes at him, reflecting back not himself but a pleasure dome with parklands and a small gazebo all of his own. When his reverie was broken by his wife's ponderous tread and her infernal "Peckie, my love?" he gave a great groan and slipped the price of freedom into his pocket.

13

It was standing room only in the court and the jurymen looked very self-important as they took their seats. It was rumored that the king himself might pay a visit and, although he never actually showed up, a small box was kept empty for his use. The first dispute was about the head, for Uncle Frank too was to be tried for colluding in his own head's removal and there had already been much discussion as to whether or not he should be openly displayed in the courtroom. Some argued that the sight would be too upsetting for the ladies, but from the ladies' objections it was clear that they would be more upset if Colonel Towneley, about whom they had heard so much, remained hidden. The clerk of the court hesitated, looking to Peckersniff for guidance.

The Lord Chief Justice, two handkerchiefs at his nose today, didn't care either way. All he wanted was silence in the court. "Oh, very well, very well I say. Put out the head," he ordered impatiently. There would be no peace until this was done.

There were gasps as Uncle Frank appeared. Mrs. Ffrench and Mabel, who were in the body of the court, sat a little straighter and Lady Widdrington, who was sitting right at the front of the gallery above, gave a shrill kind of whistle. But nobody fainted, for Frank's head looked rather fine on its horsehair base. What was more, he had such an intelligent look in his eyes that several times during the morning Peckersniff inadvertently found himself addressing him directly.

Proceedings began. Alice was to be tried first and the charges against her were read out by a pompous young clerk. However, the charges were so badly framed that she couldn't honestly plead guilty and waxed very indignant as she was sent back to the holding cell during a short refreshment recess. "I didn't conspire against either the king's majesty or his person," she complained to Hew and Dan. "I never heard such a thing. I'll plead guilty to theft but nothing else."

They nodded encouragement at her. All three had been imprisoned together in Newgate for nearly a fortnight before their trial began and during that time Hew's regard for Alice had grown tenfold, for she had comported herself with admirable fortitude and common sense. An outside observer might have thought her brazen or rash as she teased the prisoners in neighboring cells with more wit and spirit than either Dan or Hew could muster. The whole prison had heard her too, as she whiled away the hours with unlikely stories of rescues and resurrection. The guards found her almost cheeky.

But in those dead hours of the night, when the icy chill had made her bones ache and the groans echoing off the walls brought her worst nightmares to life, her courage had often failed her, and Hew and Dan had stayed by her while she sobbed quietly. "Will it be terrible, what they do to us?" she had asked again and again. "I'm not brave. I don't want to die." They had tried to reassure her and warm her, but usually failed at both.

It was a relief, in many ways, that the trial had started, even though Alice could not help flinching when the usher's voice boomed to summon her back once the break was over.

Hew hugged her. "You're as brave as a lion," he said, "and a credit to your uncle. The jury will surely see you meant no harm." Dan said the same, but their encouragement was forced. After she had gone, they were awkward with each other, each dreaming their private dreams in which the other, most certainly, did not feature.

By the time Alice was back in the dock, the witnesses had lined up and she saw Major Slavering, arms crossed, licking his lips like a dog-fox anticipating a feast. Alice gave him a look of queenly disgust.

The witnesses were many and all had seen the same thing. The accused, Alice Towneley, had stolen the head of her uncle, Colonel Francis Towneley, from the top of Temple Bar. She had then run off with it and, while doing so, had caused an affray in Grosvenor Square and later in Lincoln's Inn Fields. She had also stolen a mount rightly belonging to Kingston's Light Horse and in their individual and collective opinion, for all her angelic looks—Alice squirmed at this point—she was as wicked as any highwayman and worse.

The jury took only moments to find her guilty as charged and Peckersmith had no option but to prepare himself for the sentence. He tried not to think of Lady Widdrington's bracelet bribe, but just as he reached sadly for his black cap Alice finally lost her temper and shot to her feet. "Now look here!" she cried before anybody could stop her, "I just wanted to bury my uncle Frank properly. Is that treason? The king took my uncle's life, but what on earth can he achieve by flaunting his dead head? My goodness me"—she got that phrase from her mother—"what century are we living in? Civilization is our watchword"—that was from her father—"yet we still chop people up and use their poor bodies as flags." Quite ignorant of court etiquette, she turned on the jurymen. "Haven't any of you got uncles or aunts, or any relations for that matter? Would you be happy to see their heads pecked by birds on top of Temple Bar? I mean, even if you didn't like them, they surely deserve better than that. I only did what any of you would have done. Look at my uncle Frank." The jurymen swiveled around and found Frank looking suitably contrite. Major Slavering leaned forward, enjoying the show. "I loved him." Alice's voice was a little choked now. "That's why I did it. If the king was here, I'd tell him that. Only he's not." She sat down with a thump.

There was great whispering among the jury. Many of them thought about their uncles and aunts. Then one was pushed toward Peckersniff. "We think, possibly, mercy, Your Honor," he murmured. "Not the drop. She's very young." That juryman can never have known how very nearly he was kissed. The bracelet sparkled again in Peckersniff's mind. But only for a moment. The jury were likely to be much harder on the captain. Nevertheless, if they had already lost their appetite for executions, Hew Ffrench might yet be lucky. He asked Alice to stand and, to conceal his relief, spoke to her with all the severity of his office. "Mistress Towneley, you are guilty as charged," he said, "but mercy has been recommended by a jury of your peers. I therefore do not sentence you to execution, but rather banish you from London.

Indeed, you are to go back to your family's home, which, I understand, is in Lancashire, and once there you are to remain within five miles of its front door for at least ten years. You must go there right now. Do you understand?"

Alice understood, but she was not finished. "Well, thank you very much, but I'm not going right now," she declared. "I'm going to wait for my friends." Ignoring the soldiers, she climbed out of the dock in a manner not at all ladylike and went quite deliberately to sit beside a bristling Mabel. She could hear Major Slavering grinding his teeth but she would not look at him.

Peckersniff pinned his handkerchief more firmly to his face. "Next," he called faintly.

Hew was brought in, his legs in shackles, his clothes a disgrace, and his eyes red and rheumy. From his expression, however, he might have been going to a ball. One of the guards had told him of Alice's sentence and he was light-headed with joy. Whatever happened to Dan and himself, at least she was safe and would soon be home, under her father's care. As he climbed into the dock, Hew smiled broadly at Uncle Frank. But something in Frank's demeanor advised caution and, indeed, when Hew looked around his smile faded. Up in the gallery, Major Slavering, enraged by Alice's easy escape, was busy expounding his erstwhile captain's many iniquities to an audience not unwilling to listen, and although Alice, now sitting straight in front of him, appeared utterly confident and even Mabel seemed cautiously optimistic, it was clear from his mother's face that she, at least, was expecting the worst.

His mother turned out to be right. Slavering had done his work well. The evidence against Hew was damning. He had, by his actions, expressed sympathy with the Jacobite cause and he was responsible for the loss of the king's property. Some witnesses swore blind they had heard Hew urging Alice to flee. Others, with their own eyes, had seen him hide the head. Yet more could vouch for his treasonable thoughts because, after the battle of Culloden, he had told them to spare the wounded specifically so that they could live to fight against King George another day. The witnesses grew more and more fanciful and although the jurymen clearly disbelieved some of the wilder claims—one man swore that Hew really *was* Bonnie Prince Charlie—that only made the lesser charges more credible. It was, at any rate, indisputable that Hew had allowed two criminals to escape. Even Hew did not deny this.

Peckersniff could feel the bracelet slipping away. Then he had a brainwave. "Maybe, Captain Ffrench, the girl affected your judgment?" he asked deliberately slowly, to allow Hew time to see the bait. "Have you been led astray, young man? If Alice Towneley, as comely a wench as I have ever seen, has obliged you to do things that you would not, in your right mind, otherwise have done, this may be taken into account." At this, both Major Slavering's ribald laughter and Lady Widdrington's cackle shook the rafters, but despite Mabel muttering, "Say yes, you weak fool, admit it," Hew said nothing. Peckersniff could do no more. A guilty verdict was now inevitable.

When the jury pronounced it, Alice shot up again, but Mabel pinched her until she sat down. "You'll only make it worse," she snarled. "How I wish Hew had never met you. I'd like to execute you myself." Her mother had to hold the bench to stop herself collapsing.

Peckersniff felt sorry for them, but sorrier for himself, and he would not look at Lady Widdrington. He passed the awful sentence gazing at the floor. Even now, he tried to do his best for Hew and just sentence him to hang, but the public gallery, pumped and primed by Slavering, was having none of that. It was only right that Hew should suffer the same fate as the man whose head he had helped to steal. The scene grew so noisy that Dan could hear it from his cell. He knew what it meant. He had heard it before and when Hew, gray as prison porridge, was brought back, Dan took him from the rough grasp of the guard and sat him gently on the floor. Neither could speak, but Dan took Hew's hand and shook it hard before being dragged up to the courtroom himself.

When Dan reached the dock, Mabel and Mrs. Ffrench were clinging to each other and Alice, now a shrunken and forlorn figure, had drawn her knees up under her chin. Above, a frenziedly animated Lady Widdrington kept bawling something at the Lord Chief Justice and, for reasons Dan could not fathom, kept shaking not her fist but her wrist. Peckersniff's handkerchief had risen so far up his face that his eyes were barely visible, and anyway they were shut. This was a nightmare.

The usher saved the day by banging on the floor so hard that the vibrations made Uncle Frank's teeth clack and the pitchy hair flop over his face. As silence fell once more, Dan gazed sorrowfully at the head and itched to tidy it up, for he was a professional still. But now he had to concentrate.

"Dan Skinslicer?" the clerk asked him. "Hangman and jobbing executioner?"

"I am," said Dan.

The crowd shushed at each other as their skin crept with delicious horror. A real live hangman in the dock! A man who made a living strangling, slicing, burning, or flaying. Surely he must be a monster? It was disconcerting to find somebody who looked like the sort of husband every decent mother might wish for her daughter.

Peckersniff reopened his eyes. At least he knew what to do with this one. The City of London was currently short of men who could hang, draw, and quarter without making a complete mess of the thing. He knew it and he was sure the jurymen had been told. There would surely be witnesses lined up to prove this simpleton not guilty.

Dan answered every question politely and as accurately as he could, since he had seen too much death to be afraid of it. Yes, he had helped Alice to escape with the head. Yes, he had ridden Major Slavering's horse without the major's permission. "And he is a very good horse, Your Honor and honored jury members," Dan said. "I took a very good horse." He was so calm and accommodating that Peckersniff began to sweat. This dunderhead was going to send himself to the very gallows from which he was supposed to be saved. Then a man ran in clutching Johanna and the jury breathed again. The wife! She would surely cry heartrending tears and plead for him?

But within moments it was clear that if anybody was going to send Dan to the gallows it was Johanna. In fact, Dan hardly recognized her, for she was plump and round and dressed from head to toe in scarlet satin, imported in great rolls from France by her new smuggler lover. She had been delighted when the court messenger turned up. Nothing would suit better than to play the desolate wife for a fat fee and at first she had meant to. However, her natural ill temper soon got the better of her and, despite her silks and her painted lips, she began to berate Dan like a fishwife, calling him every name under the sun. Even Peckersniff himself could not bring her diatribe to an end, though he used his best frown. The courtroom, which at first found Johanna funny, grew bored and began calling out. Alice wanted to shout too, but her voice would not obey her anymore. She looked only at Uncle Frank. How had it come to this? He looked back at her, but his expression was a mystery.

The usher beat the walls again. "Silence in the court," he roared. The noise abated a little, but simmered, still ready to blow.

Peckersniff, at his wits' end, addressed Johanna himself. "My dear lady," he said, picking his words with care, "you have clearly had a great deal to put up with."

"Aye. I should never have married the stupid numbskull. He conned me, pretending he was clever and able to provide a lady with the good things in life."

Peckersniff sat up. "Are you saying that your husband is a very stupid man?"

"Aye. The stupidest. He's so stupid that when we married it was me who 'ad to find the parson and all. He's so stupid that sometimes he even forgets to grab a tip from those he tops. Stupid? Lord Justice, sir, 'e's stupider than your big toe."

Peckersniff circled her like a pointer. "Yes, my dear, I see, I see. Very stupid. So stupid that you have to think of everything?"

"Everything."

"So stupid that he can't even make a decent living from hanging people?"

"Even that stupid."

"Thank you, madam, you may step down."

Thoroughly pleased with herself, Johanna left the box.

Peckersniff turned at once to the jurymen. "You heard the lady," he said. "As this man's wife, she surely knows him better than any person living and we hear from her own lips, my good sirs, from her own lips, that the major sin of this wretched hangman is not treachery but stupidity! He could no more plan something than fly. He's a dolt, a dim-wit, an absolute block of wood, one of those unfortunates to whom intelligence is unknown." The crowd rustled uneasily. Where was this going? Peckersniff shook his head, oozing regret. "My good fellows," he declared at last, with a pained smile, "we cannot execute the dolts and the dimwits, or who on earth would be left?"

The crowd hummed and hawed. Gaining confidence, Peckersniff flowed smoothly on. "This man was, in my humble estimation, dragged into this unfortunate affair by mistake and was not clever enough to get himself out. In view of this, we must drop the case against him. Indeed, there is no case. I feel this most strongly." There was a groan of disappointment. "But," Peckersniff continued brightly, "we can still punish him in another way. We will make it his duty to execute Captain Hew Ffrench. Is justice not neat sometimes, is it not neat I say? Captain Ffrench will meet his Maker in three days. Three days. That should give both him and Dan Skinslicer time to prepare. That's the end of that. Now, there's just time to try this head before we all go home."

Dan was released and told to make himself scarce.

The charges against Uncle Frank were heard. He was declared to have connived in his own stealing by keeping his eyes open. The Lord Chief Justice was obliged to ask the colonel if he would close them. Uncle Frank did nothing. He was asked again. Still nothing. So he was duly found guilty of contempt of court and condemned to be put back onto Temple Bar.

As soon as he had passed this last sentence, Peckersniff declared the courtroom closed and fled. In the safety of his library, he threw his handkerchief into the fire and, after much pacing about, got out the bracelet, wrapped it up, and prepared to send it back to Lady Widdrington.

Then he heard a weighty thud, thud, thud. "Peckie, my angel," his wife trilled. "I've something to sho-o-o-o-w you!"

He cowered but there was no escape. Into the room strode Lady Peckersmith, magnificently triangular except for a pair of square feet. She came close to her husband, then closer. Her mouth opened and a blast of breath, not whiffy pig but now even whiffier wild boar, rapidly altered the Lord Chief Justice's perspective. The bracelet was his only hope! When at last he escaped from his wife's embrace, he tore up his letter to Lady Widdrington, popped the package into a pouch marked "Important Papers: KEEP OUT!" and headed for the door.

Alice had not fled the courtroom. She had hardly moved at all. She felt as if she was crying loudly and would have been surprised to be told that she was completely silent. It had all been for nothing. Hew was to die for nothing. She did not know where to turn now. Mabel had urged Mrs. Ffrench away, forbidding

Alice to come anywhere near them, and she could not bear to go back to her grandmother's. The thought of Hew alone in his prison cell was unbearable. And the most terrible thing of all was that she couldn't bear to be with Dan either, knowing what he must do. Eventually she was shoved out by the usher and she wandered the streets alone. Her moment of fame had come and gone and she was no longer of any interest to anybody.

Except to Dan, who had been patiently waiting. He did not approach Alice immediately but never let her out of his sight. His heart wept for her, and sometimes his eyes too. Occasionally she would draw herself up and Dan knew that she was thinking of some plan—rushing to the king, storming New-gate Prison, setting fire to the gallows, or some such. This tortured him more, for when the plan was abandoned, Alice's desolation ran deeper than ever. Eventually, she found herself back under Temple Bar and sat stiffly on an old bench. When Dan edged closer and then tentatively sat down beside her, he was relieved that she did not recoil. He knew he was once again a hangman in her eyes but she had nobody else.

"What have I done, Dan Skinslicer?" she asked, wincing for the first time ever at his name. "Captain Ffrench is really dying for me."

"Captain Ffrench chose his own path," Dan told her. "Blaming yourself is silly."

"Maybe I am silly."

"No," said Dan slowly. "You are many things, missy. Bossy sometimes, even hurtful. But you are never silly—at least I've never seen it."

"You don't know me very well then," Alice said, hunching her legs up. The face she turned to Dan was streaked and, as the daylight faded, he could almost see through her. They sat in silence. Then Alice put out her hand and touched Dan's shoulder. "I'm sorry," she said, and her voice broke. In a moment she was folded into two strong arms and Dan rocked back and forth as she wept and wept. "You do know me, Dan Skinslicer," she sobbed. "You know me better than Hew Ffrench. He loves me. I can see that. But he doesn't know me. He can't, because his eyes are full of that kind of love-blindness people get. Do you know what I mean?" Dan nodded, unable to speak himself now. Alice wiped her eyes on his sleeve. "Hew's not like you. You see just me, Alice Towneley, a foolish girl who has got you into trouble. But Hew, well, Hew sees somebody else, somebody almost perfect, and it's not me, it's really not me, although I can't help loving him for thinking it is." She sobbed harder than ever. "But I can hardly bear it, Dan Skinslicer, because this blind love has sent him to your gallows. If I'd been fat

197

and hairy, he'd never have even dreamed of helping me, let alone loving me. And just look where it's led."

Dan held her close. Her hair was lank and greasy but it was the dearest thing in the world to him. She had that capacity, this Alice, to make him happier, angrier, more elated, more frustrated, more like a lion or more like a worm than any other person he had ever met. And she was right. His sort of love was not like Hew's. He did not think her perfect. He did not even think her good. He just thought of her as somebody for whom he would gladly lay down his life. Dan's love did not depend on the blue of Alice's eyes, although it was a wonder to him. Nor did it depend on her loving him, for Dan thought this impossible. The truth was that his love did not depend on anything at all. It was just there, lifting him up or casting him down as it chose, but never waning or diminishing. It was so steady that sometimes he wondered if it had disappeared, but then realized that it could no more disappear than his own skin could disappear. It was just part of him.

He did not stop rocking until Alice stopped sobbing, and then he found a grubby bit of handkerchief on which she could blow her nose. They sat in silence again. Alice looked at the top of the Bar, wondering how she had ever dared climb so high. "Will they put Uncle Frank up there tonight?" she whispered.

"No." Dan shook his head. "He has to wait until. . ." His voice petered out.

Alice pinched his arm as hard as Mabel had pinched hers. "You'll not let Hew suffer, will you, Dan Skinslicer? Please don't let him suffer."

"I promise on my mother's grave," said Dan quietly. Hew would certainly not suffer, not for a moment. If Dan could make sure of anything, he could make sure of that.

As evening fell, he managed to ease Alice away from Temple Bar and back to Lady Widdrington's. She resisted, but Dan was firm. "The king's justices'll not come after you until after Captain Hew is . . . has gone," he said. 'But you must stay out of sight."

Alice looked over her shoulder, fearful. "But I must be on Kennington Common on Thursday," she said. "I can't just abandon Hew now."

"I don't want you there, but I suppose I'd want to do the same," he said doubtfully.

"Thank you for understanding." Alice huddled next to him as he knocked on the door. It was opened by Ursula. First her wig, then her nose, then the rest of her peeked around. The sight of her aunt's silly affectations made Alice's heart shrink further. "Don't leave me here, Dan Skinslicer," she whimpered, wrapping her arms as far as they would go around his rock-like frame. "I feel safer when I'm with you."

Dan peeled her arms off with weary regret. "I can't take you where I have to go, missy. You know that."

"Yes," whispered Alice, "I know."

Ursula darted between them and, before Alice could say anything else, she whipped Alice inside and slammed the door. At once Dan walked away and tried not to look back. But when, unable to resist, he did look, the shutters were being none too gently closed, telling him very firmly that he was not wanted there. Before the last of the light was blocked out, he thought he could hear Alice's heart breaking and very nearly ran to her again. But it was not the right thing to do. He resisted and walked on.

At the corner of the square he leaned against the railings. He leaned a long time, his head filled with emotions he could not control and some he could not understand. Once Captain Ffrench was dead, a calculating voice told him, it was not impossible that Alice might come to love him. A warmer voice, more familiar, scoffed. She'll never love you, Dan Skinslicer. And anyway, you are already married. No, no, the first voice continued. Your wife is divorcing you. You could be a free man. The second voice urged him not to dream.

Dan put his hands over his ears. "I am just an executioner with a job to do," he muttered to himself, and, with a huge effort of will, began to concentrate not on Alice but on that. He walked slowly for a while. Once he stopped and glared at some street urchins. They stuck out their tongues. But Dan did not even see them. He walked for a little longer before he suddenly changed direction and, with unusual speed and decision, headed for the city. He needed to start collecting the tools of his trade. He would need good ones. Maybe he could even find some of his old ones. But before he began looking, he would turn off and make a different kind of call. Dan Skinslicer had had an idea.

14

On Thursday morning, execution morning, the heat came with the dawn. Londoners prepared themselves for a roasting carnival day. Some highborn ladies organized hampers to take and filled them with pigeon pie, sliced mutton, and currant tarts. Servants groaned as they were presented with great baskets stashed with cider, ale, and wine, which they were expected to carry to where their master and mistress wished to sit. Children sulked when told by their mothers that they couldn't come, only to whoop and cheer when the order was rescinded by their fathers, who, although feeling queasy themselves, nevertheless felt honor-bound to say, as their fathers had before them, that a good execution never did anybody any harm. Those further down the social scale decorated their caps and hats and wrapped their bread and cheese in flannel cloths. Tradesmen polished their horses and loaded their carts. Pickpockets put on their baggiest trousers.

From early on, people began to pour over the bridge toward Kennington Common and to flock around the gibbet, pointing out the bloodstains left by previous miscreants and laughing at Uncle Frank's head, brought to "witness" the end of Captain Hew Ffrench. Some youths, anxious to impress, climbed up to the gibbet crossbar and sat swinging their legs. They were much admired by young ladies on the ground. One stripped off his shirt and gave a passable imitation of a condemned man, reveling in the horrified groans as he pretended to hang himself. Then he slipped and very nearly did hang himself. After that he slithered down, laughing too loudly, and contented himself with shouting at Dan, who was busy checking that everything was in order.

Alice had arrived early and alone, leaving her grandmother singing nursery rhymes in the drawing room. Ursula, to Alice's relief, was purposefully still in bed. Alice's preoccupation with executions was, in her aunt's opinion, unhealthy and possibly catching. It was hard for Alice to know where to stand, but in the end she chose a place at the front, between two fishwives.

By the time Hew appeared, kneeling in a cart and guarded by a squadron of his former fellow soldiers, the noose already around his neck, the crowd was very merry. Up on the scaffold, Dan set out his instruments as the law dictated. The sun was well up now, but neither Dan nor Hew really noticed. Of the two, Hew was the more relaxed. There is something about going to your death, he found, that had, mercifully, a slightly unreal quality. The noise of the merrymaking rang in his ears but did not pierce the innermost recesses of his brain. In there, right at the kernel, he was reunited with Marron and riding in line at the beginning of the battle of Culloden, his sword held steady in its half-basket grip. On that day, in the face of enemy fire, he had remained true to his men and himself. He could do it again. Unconsciously, he knelt a little taller.

As they watched the sorry procession, many women in the crowd who had come to jeer found themselves praying instead. Hew's youth and the frank expression on his face reminded them that this boy was somebody's son. If luck had been different, maybe he could have been theirs. Some dropped their eyes. Others allowed their grubby children to throw rotten potatoes but were glad when they missed the target.

In keeping with the tradition of condemned men, Hew had spent the previous evening composing letters to his mother and to Alice and now turned his mind to the letters again. They had not been easy to write, but he had felt it very important that his mother should·

know that he did not hold Alice in any way responsible for his death. "I chose my own path," he had written. "I'm only sorry that I never had a chance to explain. But then I know I don't need to, especially not to you. Be comforted that I did the right thing and that is what counts in the end." He had finished the letter with regrets at not having been a more helpful son and regretted too, more than his own life, the trouble that the manner of his passing would undoubtedly cause to hers.

To Alice, he had written only this:

My dear Miss Alice Towneley, we have had an extraordinary acquaintance, you and I. I cannot be sorry that I met you and I hope, whatever your future brings, that you will never forget that you once filled the heart of
   Hew Elliot Ffrench
   lately a Captain, Kingston's Light Horse

As he drew nearer the scaffold, however, Hew could no longer keep what was about to happen to him at a safe distance and he found himself unexpectedly glad of the merrymakers. Their presence and their shouting added grit to his determination to make a good death. If he quailed inside, he would not let them see. He clenched his fists. Occasionally, when the cart bumped over a stone and he was thrown sideways, he found himself staring directly into people's faces. It was the sympathetic rather than the hostile eyes that caused him the most trouble. He could not afford to acknowledge pity. If he did, he would be lost. As soon as he was able, he looked only ahead.

The crowd was at its thickest where a barrier had been erected both to give Dan a little breathing space in which to perform his duties and to prevent any friend of Hew's from running forward to swing on his legs once he was strung up. The whole point was that Hew should be alive when the disemboweling began.

Dan was sweating. He was pleased with the tools he had managed to procure and, although he always kept his implements meticulously honed, he tested them constantly, for it was particularly important that they should be keen today. Shielding his eyes, he scanned the crowd, unsure where Alice would be standing. At last he saw her on his left, a small figure almost crushed between the two slab-faced wifeys. He nodded at her but she could not nod back.

Drums rolled as Hew's escort approached the barrier leaving Hew to pass through alone. Major Slavering clicked his tongue, annoyed. He wanted the escort to go right up to the scaffold. But it was too late now. He barked at his men to stay in line and turn their horses to witness the punishment of their former officer. The cornet had already shut his eyes.

Dan came down to help Hew out of the cart and found his victim's hands steadier than his own. Hew tried to joke that Dan had better take some deep breaths or he would cut the kind of jaggedy line that he complained of in others. Dan didn't respond.

As they climbed up onto the platform, Hew was assailed by waves of clammy panic. He tried hard to remove himself once again from the present and he searched his mind for that picture of himself on Marron. Where was it, now that he really needed it? Why would it not flood his brain, soothing as brandy, and get him through the worst? But all Hew could see was the glint of Dan's knives and the dull edge of the ax and all he could hear was Dan repeatedly muttering, "Forgive me for what I am going to do, forgive me."

"Of course I forgive you!" Hew was surprised and alarmed that Dan, who had executed hundreds of men, should lose his professional detachment at this crucial moment. "Just do it properly, Dan Skinslicer. That's all I ask."

A trumpet sounded. It was time. Hew faced the crowd with Dan behind him. He could feel Dan pick up the long end of the rope down his back, releasing a little of the pressure on his neck, for the rope was heavy. The disemboweling table waited, like a bed without a mattress. As a gesture, Dan had draped it in red cloth so that Hew's blood would not show so badly, but the red simply drew attention to Dan's cold implements. Hew could already feel them, freshly minted, each waiting to tweak at his flesh in its own particular deadly way. Over the top of the crowd, the jurymen who had condemned him were eating roast grouse and chatting to their wives. Hew searched for Lord Chief Justice Peckersniff, but he was missing. *He probably had something more important to do,* thought Hew bitterly. In the field behind the carriages, every blade of grass appeared a different green and Hew wondered why he had never before seen that grass is speckled. He should have been a painter, not a soldier! Everything seemed so clear, clearer than it had ever been, as if layers of gauze had been stripped from his eyes. No man could have devised such a torture as this. Just when he wished to see nothing, he could see everything, and there was nobody in the world with whom to share it. The loneliness was indescribable.

It was not until Dan tightened the noose that Hew caught sight of Alice. Her pinched face nearly killed him. He could feel his knees buckle as their eyes met for a second. *Help me, Alice,* he silently begged, all his courage finally deserting him.

And she did. She could not see his eyes as clearly as he could see hers, but she knew, instinctively, what was wanted. Throwing back the hood of her cloak, she stood in full view. She could not smile any encouragement, but she could look, and in her look Hew found his strength. Forgetting Marron and Culloden, it was Alice's steadfast face that he kept before him as he stepped up on to the stool and waited for the awful jerk.

Contrary to what she was expecting to do, Alice did not scrunch her eyes shut when the final moment came. She saw Dan secure the rope and knock away the stool. She saw Hew's head snap back. She watched him flail. It was dreadful to her, but she carried on watching just in case, up there against the vaulting darkness, his breath fighting a heaving, hopeless battle and his legs kicking and kicking to find some miraculous purchase in the air, Hew could still see her. She knew this was well nigh impossible, but she would watch just in case, just in case. Mourning, weeping, and the vale of tears would come later. This was what she could do for him now.

The hanging was over in a moment and Dan cut Hew down with a swing and a vehemence that Alice found disturbing. She supposed it was because Dan wanted Hew dead as quickly as possible, but walloping his body so that it hurtled to the ground behind the table and had to be manhandled back up again was not what Hew deserved. The crowd booed and Dan had to slow down. He showed them his knife and they began to cheer up. At the first cut, Hew seemed to twitch and shiver, then suddenly, ignoring the crowd, Dan worked with speedy efficiency, his knives soon tarnished and his hands red. The "drawing" was quickly over and the fire began to crackle with its fleshy fuel, but Alice still looked, for she had temporarily lost all control over herself. *Look away, look away*, her head cried, but it was as if she had been hypnotized. Only when Dan raised his great ax did the muscles in her legs dissolve, and by the time the ax crashed down and Dan held Hew's head aloft, dangling from its dark hair, Alice toppled over and passed out.

Three things happened at once. Dan did not quarter Hew's body but flung it into a coffin and nailed down the lid with a dozen determined bangs. As he did so, Mrs. Ffrench, who had been standing on the right, her face covered to make sure Hew did not recognize her, approached, leaning heavily on Mabel. They would take the body away. Then, the crowd parted to allow a messenger through. The king, who wanted no more trouble with heads, had changed his mind. Hew's head should not be displayed on Temple Bar, nor Uncle Frank's, nor anyone else's ever again. Alice's escapade had ended that tradition. It was a pity, but there it was.

From now on, traitors would be buried with all their bits together. Under this new dispensation, the head of Colonel Frank Towneley should be put back in its hatbox and given to Miss Alice Towneley to take home with her and good riddance to both. Hew Ffrench's head, which the justice tried not to look at as it sat on the planks at Dan's feet, dripping unmentionable matter slowly through the chinks, should be put in the coffin with the body. The justice was commissioned to see that this was done.

But Dan, to Mrs. Ffrench's horror, looked mutinous. "I'm not opening the coffin for anybody," he said, standing with his great arms crossed. "It's not right."

"Don't be impertinent, Mr. Skinslicer," said the justice. "It's on the orders of the king."

"I don't care. I fill coffins and I shut them. I don't open them. Captain Ffrench's head can go in with Colonel Towneley's." He leaned down, picked Hew's head up, and popped it into Frank's hatbox, with Frank's on top. The hatbox was almost too full, but Dan squashed it down.

The justice stepped backward, fanning himself. The smell from the fire where the bowels were still burning was both acrid and sickly. Dan loomed over him. "It's bad luck, see, to open a coffin. Have you never heard? The dead become undead and haunt you." The justice moaned.

211

"Don't be ridiculous." Mabel's voice broke through, sharp as an icicle. "Open the coffin at once, man. The least you can do for my brother, after such a clumsy execution, is to allow his body to rest in wholesome dignity. What a disgraceful performance."

Mrs. Ffrench added her pleas more quietly and sweetly, but just as vehemently, to those of her daughter.

They were still arguing when Alice was woken by the smell of mackerel. The fishwives were flapping their aprons over her. She only gradually regained her senses and for at least five minutes everything was a muddle. Then it became horribly clear. She stumbled away from the fishwives, feeling as if she had been disemboweled herself. *I am quite hollow*, she thought. *I'll never feel anything again.*

There was nowhere to go but the scaffold and she crawled up behind Mabel, who was quarreling with Dan with increasing intensity. But Dan, his hands still stained, was implacable. "I won't do it," he was saying. "Not for anyone. If the king wants the coffin opened, he'll have to do it himself. Or you do it." The justice looked helplessly about him.

"I will do it," said Mabel, and Dan stepped aside but offered Mabel no tools, and though she scraped her fingers and almost cried with vexation, the lid remained firmly fixed. Now Mrs. Ffrench was on her knees, renewing her pleadings.

Dan shifted uncomfortably. "I can't do it, mistress," he said. "No executioner would. It's against everything we stand for. You don't really want to see inside there, do you?"

"Is it money you want?" asked Mrs. Ffrench tremulously.

At this Dan's face grew quite pink. "I do not, madam," he retorted. "Now, if you will excuse me, you must tell me where you wish the body to be taken and I will make sure it arrives safely."

"We're not going anywhere until Hew's head is in the coffin too." Mabel stamped both feet. "I thought he was your friend!"

"And I can't go until I have seen the king's orders carried out." The justice was almost as desperate as Mrs. Ffrench. This great vegetable of a hangman! He would have words about him.

Alice edged her way farther onto the platform and when Mabel saw her, her venom increased. "Why are you here?" She jabbed a finger into Alice's chest. "We hate you. Hate you. Because of you my brother is dead and my mother and I will end up in the gutter. I don't know how on earth you persuaded Hew to help you in your ludicrous scheme, but I hope you are satisfied. And now, to add insult upon insult, this hulking imbecile won't even put Hew's head with his body. Some friends you are."

Alice raised her eyes miserably to Dan. "Couldn't you . . ."

"NO!"

Alice continued to stare at him long after she had quite understood what he was saying.

The crowd was dispersing, trudging back into the city. Soon, the only people left were a dozen small boys reenacting what they had just witnessed. Above the coffin, the severed rope was lazily unraveling.

"We surely can't stay here forever," the justice groaned. If he had to stay even a moment longer, he would be ill. It was one thing handing out a capital sentence, quite another having to look at the consequences.

Alice sat him down. "Do you actually have to witness the head going in with the body yourself?" she asked. "Couldn't you just say it has been done? Perhaps I could witness it for you."

Mabel almost boxed Alice's ears. "Of course you can't witness it. That's this man's job," she cried. "Now get this coffin opened at once."

But the justice sensed some sympathy from Alice and resolved only to address her in future. He unrolled his order. "No, no, you're right, young lady. It doesn't actually say I should witness it absolutely myself *personally*," he said doubtfully. "It doesn't at all. See, here."

Alice saw. "Well then," she said, "leave it to me. My uncle Frank's head was brought along here as a witness, so I think it only right that he finishes his duties by witnessing Captain Ffrench's head going into the coffin. That would make everything right, wouldn't it, and you can tell your fellow justices that the king's orders have been carried out with perfect propriety. For they will be carried out, Mr. Justice, sir, they will be carried out, *just not here*." She finished in a whisper.

There was a hiatus as the justice hopped from foot to foot. Then, he with relief and Dan with horror, saw Major Slavering hand his reins to the cornet and spring over the grass toward them. His pleasure was unlimited and undisguised.

Wasting no more time, Dan dragged Hew's coffin across the platform and lowered it into the cart, sweeping the hatbox in too. "We'd best be getting along then," he said, poking the fire to make sure all was burning merrily.

"No, I tell you. Absolutely not. Not until my brother's head is restored to him. I refuse." Mabel stood above Dan, glowering, with Mrs. Ffrench weeping by her side.

To Mabel's fury and astonishment, Dan said nothing more, but seized her and shoved her unceremoniously on top of the coffin, where she landed in an undignified heap, and then toppled Mrs. Ffrench and Alice down like ninepins after her. At this, the justice began to wail. What was this fiendish hangman going to do next? "Major Slavering, Major Slavering," the justice sobbed, "the hangman's gone MAD!" And, indeed, Dan did look rather mad as he whipped his gallant pony into a trot.

As the pony took off, Major Slavering began to run, gesticulating and shouting, but when he got to the gallows, what with the blood and the smoldering remains, he couldn't help stopping to gloat. Oh, what sweet revenge, to see his enemy's innards cooking so beautifully. He looked after Dan, who had almost disappeared. He would follow him in a moment. Or perhaps not. After all, who really cared about a bumbling executioner when the delicious spectacle of snooty Captain two-effed French sizzling like a common fry-up was here to enjoy. He bent down and scooped up some blood in his fingers and sniffed it. Enemy gore, he remarked gleefully to the justice, what better fuel to warm the cockles of a soldier's heart. Then, finding the justice's pea-green face irresistible, he grinned and thrust his sticky red hand right under the poor man's nose. That was the end. Unable to take any more, the justice's stomach gave a large heave and he was massively sick all down Major Slavering's shiny leather boots.

Had Dan seen this, he would have found it most satisfactory, but he never looked back. Waving his bloody ax dangerously near the necks of anybody who got in the way, he urged the pony to go faster and faster. Even had Mabel wanted to carry on shouting, she could not, for she was battered against the coffin like a paper bag. In the end, she had to cling to her mother, who clung to Alice, who, in her turn, clung to the hatbox to try and prevent the heads from being catapulted out into the street. Some folk screeched at them and some, clipped by the wheel spokes, shook their fists. But Dan never wavered and the pony galloped on. As they neared Grosvenor Square, he put out a great arm and yanked Alice up beside him. "Get Bunion to open the gate at the back," he grunted, and pitched her swiftly out. Alice picked herself up and ran to the door, banging until she was let in, then flew through, crying for Bunion, or anybody, to help her. In moments, the cart was swinging inside the yard and the gates swung shut behind it.

At last the pony was allowed to halt and it stood, its head between its knees and its flanks heaving, as, to Mabel and Mrs. Ffrench's utter confusion, Dan turned his ax over and began, swiftly and urgently, to lever off the top of the coffin, just as all this time they had been asking and he had been refusing to do. The servants flapped about like jittery geese but Dan took no notice. He never looked up until the coffin lid cracked and he was able to pull it to one side. Alice couldn't breathe. Hew was dead. She had seen him die with her own eyes. What was Dan going to do now?

Dan did nothing. But then, from the coffin, slow as the unfolding of a flower, a headless body arose. The torso was rent and bloodied, but it sat up. Mabel gasped and Mrs. Ffrench would have keeled over completely had Dan not jumped down and caught her. Alice alone stood quite still, apart from a little flutter in her throat. The torso was steady for a second or two, then slumped over. Now a disheveled mop of black hair appeared from underneath it, then a head with a rope still wound tightly around its neck and, finally, a face that was certainly Hew's, sporting an expression of almost comical wonder at the dummy sitting on his lap. There was a pause before Hew draped the dummy over the side of the coffin, where the arms swung, making a dull clump, clump, clump. Then he looked about carefully, as if a sudden movement might see him plummeting once again toward Dan Skinslicer's butcher's table. Apart from a great red welt on his neck, he was white as snow.

Alice made a little sound. Like a sleepwalker, Hew turned to listen, but as he moved, the rope around his neck caught on one of the coffin nails and he began to choke. That snapped him awake and suddenly he was on his feet, eyes flashing wide as he grappled and wrenched at the twisted hemp that cut into his windpipe.

In a second Alice was beside him. She knew nothing about ropes and her fingers, so willing, almost succeeded in strangling him. It was Dan who effortlessly slipped the knot, released Hew, and tossed the noose to the ground. Blindly, Hew put out his hand and Alice took it. "Hew," she said. His name was all she could manage. "Hew." It was enough. Hew stepped out of the coffin and hugged her so tightly she thought her ribs might crack.

Mabel was absolutely livid. "What on earth is going on?" she raged. "Why were we not told? What have you been doing, Skinslicer?"

Dan, not really wanting to look at Alice and Hew, was grateful for her diversion. "I'm sorry, mistress," he said in a voice half triumphant, half apologetic, "but I daren't say anything before because I didn't know as I could pull it off."

He was interrupted by Alice. She had extricated herself from Hew and was pulling at his sleeve. "Dan Skinslicer, Dan Skinslicer"—she dazzled him with her delight—"you're a genius." And she kissed him.

Dan blushed to the roots of his hair and hurried around to the pony's head, murmuring about giving the poor animal a drink, but Mrs. Ffrench put out an arm to stop him. "Mr. Skinslicer," she said, "I'm so startled I hardly know anything anymore, but I do know that you must be the bravest of the brave. What would the justices have done to you if you had been caught? How can we ever thank you? You have saved my son." She seemed set to collapse again. "We can never repay you."

Dan helped her onto the steps. "I don't want paying, mistress," he said. "I did it for—well, I just did it." Mrs. Ffrench nodded at him. She knew.

"You still should have told us." Mabel was furious with her mother for her undiluted gratitude. "For goodness' sake, all of us could have been sentenced to hang if you really had been forced to open the coffin in front of the justice—which, by the way, you should have been."

But Dan was not going to be bullied by Mabel. He shrugged her away.

Now Hew caught his hand and Dan was so embarrassed that Alice had to come to his rescue. "Who made the dummy?" she asked, dancing about like a ten-year-old. "And where did you get all the blood and guts from?" She was impossible to resist.

"Well, I went to your granny's wigmaker," Dan told her. "I'm afraid I was not very nice to him, but I did at least pay him," he went on pointedly. "Anyway, I got him to make a body and a very nice waxen head—I chose the wig myself."

"But swapping them in front of all those people—"
Alice stopped dancing. Dan had made stealing Uncle
Frank look like child's play.

"I knew that I would only have a second to make the
change between Captain Ffrench and the dummy—"
Dan didn't get a chance to finish.

"Which is why you bumped poor Hew so heavily
onto the floor of the scaffold," Alice interrupted, her
thrill at Dan's astonishing courage mixed with the delicious terror of retrospect.

"That's right, missy." Dan grinned. "That was the
crucial bit. I had to make it look like a bit of an error.
Anyhow, I managed to get the captain into the coffin and
get the dummy onto the table before anybody volun-
teered to come and help. I was frightened, though, that
the captain would land flat on the dummy so that I
couldn't get it out, but luckily he landed on his side
so I could get a decent hold and slip the dummy over
him. And those soldiers standing at the sides, not at
the back behind the scaffold—that was another piece
of luck. I hadn't really thought of them." He cracked
his knuckles. "Thank goodness though, or I might have
chickened out. But anyway, it was quick, quick onto
the table with the dummy for the slicing." Dan looked
at Hew. "Pig," he said. Hew looked a little startled.
"No, no," Dan explained. "It was a bag of pig's innards
that I got the wigmaker to sew into the dummy's

stomach and into your head. Lots of blood and guts. Worked a treat."

"And you even remembered to put a rope around the dummy's neck," said Alice, so full of admiration she thought she might take off. "You thought of everything."

"Well, nearly everything," said Dan modestly. "I did remember to make air holes in the coffin so as the poor captain could breathe, but look at your breeches, sir." Hew looked down. "They're brown," Dan said. "Now look at the dummy's."

"They're black!" exclaimed Alice, her jig momentarily suspended.

"I couldn't remember what color they were," said Dan. "Just fancy. All that time in Newgate together and I couldn't remember the color of a pair of breeches. Probably because it was so dark. Anyway, I only realized my mistake when you were hanging. A nasty moment." Dan's grin faded. "But it's over now."

A voice from the back door brought them all up short. "What is this? A fairground?" Lady Widdrington was gazing down and she recognized Mrs. Ffrench. "Good Lord, madam," she called. "I thought you were a lady, not a tradesman. I never expected to find you at the back door."

Mrs. Ffrench went to greet her, but found herself confronted by Ursula, whose mouth was agape.

Although the execution was hardly an hour past, a friend had already been around to tell her that it was the bloodiest she had ever seen. And now to find the dead man talking in the yard! Such a good-looking dead man too. Ursula did not know whether to flirt or faint.

Alice wanted her to do neither. The appearance of her grandmother and aunt only served as a reminder that she, Dan, Hew, and Uncle Frank's head were not yet out of danger. They must leave London at once. Only at Towneley would they be safe. Behind those granite hills, nobody would come looking for them. In a week or two, when some new scandal began to circulate through the country, the saga of Uncle Frank's head would be quite forgotten. "I want to go home, Granny," she said, hoping that the firmness of her tone would keep her grandmother's mind from wandering off. "Indeed, I must go home, since that is what Justice Peckersniff told me to do and I'm never disobedient."

Her grandmother bent her head to the side. For one awful moment Alice thought that she was going to pretend that her granddaughter was a complete stranger full of ill intent and bellow for soldiers. Instinctively, Alice stepped back to protect Hew. However, Lady Widdrington just beckoned Alice to her, her little eyes both keen and sorry. "You'll not

come back to visit your Faraway Granny, I know that."
It was a statement of fact rather than a question. "No,
Granny, I won't," Alice said. It seemed a time for truth.
"I don't think I'll ever come to London again."

"I'll miss you." Lady Widdrington wiped away a
tear, then gave a cackle and signaled to Bunion to
prepare the carriage. "That is, when I remember who
you are!"

"Well, I won't be sorry," said Ursula, flumping down
the steps with her hands on her hips. Her face was half
twisted into a smile for Hew and half into a glare for
her niece. It seemed just the last insulting straw that
this chit of a girl, who had ridden with no stockings
on, should leave with not one man in tow, but two.

"Good-bye, Aunt," Alice said to her, but gave up when
Ursula flounced off.

Hew was bidding his mother and Mabel farewell.
"Look after each other," he told them. "I will send
money to you somehow."

"Go, go quickly, Hew," his mother urged. "I couldn't
bear it if anything else was to happen to you." She
shook Dan's hand warmly, speechless now in both her
happiness at her son's rescue and her grief at his
departure.

Mabel, although her good-bye to Alice was terse,
managed a warmer smile for Hew. "Write to us," she
said, and then added, for Alice's benefit, "You'll need

a new identity, but don't let those Catholics turn you into a priest."

Alice tossed her hair, rising to the bait. "Certainly not," she said, taking Hew's hand in a proprietorial gesture that made Mabel want to slap her. "I don't think Hew is destined for the Church."

"Children, children," admonished Mrs. Ffrench, "you must be friends if"—she looked directly at Hew— "you are eventually to be sisters."

Dan didn't want to hear this. He gave a small gulp and seized Hew's head. Alice screamed. But it was only Hew's hair that Dan was after. With a knife and not a little satisfaction, he began to chop off the beautiful black locks. Thick wedges formed a carpet on the ground and Hew's face was soon framed by uneven spikes. "Disguise," Dan muttered. "Sorry if it does away with your looks." He busied himself bundling the dummy back into the coffin and hammered down the nails again with a little too much enthusiasm. "You'll have to take this and bury it," he said to Mrs. Ffrench. "Bury it deep and don't forget that you'll have to do some mourning for your son. If you look too happy, we'll all be undone."

At the word "mourning," Ursula, who had flounced back, cheered up. She had some spectacular mourning clothes in which, she believed, she looked absolutely ravishing. She would lay them out at once.

"Now," Dan continued, "I'll wash under your pump and dress up in your livery if you don't mind, Lady Widdrington. Bunion here can take the cart bearing Captain Ffrench's coffin and Mrs. Ffrench and I'll drive the carriage north. We'll send it back to you somehow. Captain Ffrench, get in and keep your head down. Come on, missy, time to go." He disappeared and they heard muffled oaths before he reappeared, squeezed into white leg britches and a scarlet coat, with a white wig and a hat with an immense cockade. His face was mutinous and he dared Alice to laugh as he picked up the hatbox and pushed her toward the carriage door. Alice slipped past him one last time to plant a spontaneous kiss on the cheek of Mrs. Ffrench. "I'm sorry for all the fuss," she said, "and Uncle Frank would be sorry too. Everything seems to have happened so quickly."

"Come on now," Dan said impatiently. "The longer we dally the greater the danger. We'll just have to hope that your grandmother's servants won't gossip about what they've seen here."

Bunion sniffed. "You're not the only one with morals, Dan Skinslicer," he said. "Take care of my horses."

With that the gates swung back open and the carriage was gone. It was only when they were well out of London that Dan realized he had forgotten to put Hew's waxen effigy into the coffin. Uncle Frank's hatbox contained two heads still. It made Hew feel rather strange, to be traveling with his head in a box, but, with Alice at his side, he reckoned that he could get used to anything.

15

Alice's return home in her grandmother's carriage with a hangman, an admirer, and Uncle Frank's head was greeted with some surprise by her parents. Alice told a garbled story, to which her parents, standing awkwardly in the cavernous gloom of the great hall, appeared to be paying attention. "Yes, dear, goodness!" they both said at appropriate moments. In fact, neither heard more than every fifth word. Alice's father was wondering about the accuracy of his rain gauge, suspect ever since Alice had gone away, and her mother about the prodigious amounts of mold that one of her cheeses had sprouted. "Well, you are very welcome, er, er . . ." Sir Thomas looked vaguely at his wife.

"Captain Ffrench and Mr. Skinslicer," said Alice helpfully.

"Indeed."

"Alice, dear, we weren't quite expecting you. How's Faraway Granny—and Ursula, of course?" Her mother wondered if the cheese had grown too warm—or perhaps too cold. It reminded her—"Uncle Frank's body arrived in surprisingly good order," she said. "We buried him. It was a sad day."

Sir Thomas echoed his wife's sentiments. "Sad day, sad day," he repeated.

Now was the moment. "I've brought his head back," said Alice, pointing to Mabel's hatbox. "We should bury it too."

Lady Towneley looked at the hatbox with some disappointment, for despite her spreading waistline and collapsing beauty, she had inherited an interest in fashion from Lady Widdrington. "Oh, what a pity. I thought you were going to show me some new styles."

Alice giggled. Home was just the same. She slipped her arm through her mother's, who looked down at her daughter and sighed. "Oh well," she said. "I suppose we can combine another burial with a party for your homecoming. Such a pity Frank won't be here to enjoy it." She dabbed her eyes, for she had been very fond of her brother-in-law.

Sir Thomas gave a little hum. He too had been fond of his brother, but now it was raining. He could tell that because large drops of water were dripping from the ceiling somewhere miles above and splashing the stones at his feet. His rain gauge was calling.

"Better go, Father," Alice prompted gently. "Who knows how much water you might collect today? It could be a record."

"If you're sure." Sir Thomas did not need more persuading. "Nice to have you back, dearest daughter," he said, feeling pleased that he still liked her, "and I hope you will come and help me again at my calculations. Somehow, since you went, they have become rather dull." He waved an arm at Hew and Dan and vanished up the staircase.

The rain pattered down with increasing vehemence and, although they were certain that their beds would be damp, both Dan and Hew were delighted to hear it, for within half an hour of their arrival the roads were reduced to a quagmire. Had Bonnie Prince Charlie himself been at Towneley, it would have been difficult for even Major Slavering at his most determined to beat a path through to arrest him. Alice had the servants build up the fire and, for the first time since they had known each other, the three of them sat in a row: warm, safe, and, after Alice had nagged the cook, well fed.

Three days later, in the very early morning, several people could be seen slipping into the weather-beaten stone church that was tucked beside the house. From the outside, to fool the Protestants, it looked like a coach house, with broad doors and high windows. Indeed, several of the Towneley conveyances were parked haphazardly around about. But inside was a small chapel, smelling of polish and incense. At the far end, an altarpiece, beautifully carved with flowers and saints, was lit by candles and, in front of it, the red sanctuary lamp, like the eye of God, hung suspended. Father Saunderson, the Towneley's pet priest, was already on his knees and beside him was the hatbox.

It was chilly in the chapel and Alice and her mother pulled their cloaks around them. Dan and Hew stood in silence at the back, Dan wondering what Johanna would say if she could see him now. Hew was happier than he would ever be again in his whole life. Over the last few days, as she had shown her guests around the castle and taken them along the secret paths up onto the moors, Alice had chattered away, telling stories as they plowed through the bogs. At dinnertime, she sat demurely near her parents, flashing glances at him under her eyelashes amid the candlelight. In the chapel, with her head bowed, she looked like a medieval saint. If Hew could not find as much to say as she could, it mattered little, for Alice never ran out of conversation. When they were alone, the silences that fell between them were silky, easy things. Only the presence of Dan made things sticky and Hew could see how hard Alice worked to make this right. He loved her even more for that.

The vault under the chapel had been opened and a small, dark hole winked at them. From here Uncle Frank's coffin had already been extricated and it was sitting on top of the marble slab that marked the tomb of a previous Sir Thomas and his lady.

"Now, Father Saunderson," said Alice's father, nervous in case the weather changed while he was otherwise engaged, "let's begin."

The ceremony did not take much time. The hatbox, looking very incongruous, was set on the altar for a blessing as if it was some kind of purchase on a shop counter. Dan harrumphed, thinking Father Saunderson looked like nothing but a magician, with his cope and his incomprehensible mumblings.

Then came the moment when the coffin had to be opened. Dan was ready for the summons and did the job easily with hammer and chisel. He knew better than to look inside. Ignoring everybody, he picked up the hatbox and set it down on the tomb. He could see that Alice's mother had her handkerchief over her face and that her father was steadfastly telling his rosary beads. Father Saunderson tried to rise, but never quite made it and Hew, who had no wish to see the effigy of his own head again, hovered at a distance.

Suddenly, Alice was at Dan's side, smiling conspiratorially, as if they were the only two people in the world. "Well, Dan Skinslicer," she said, "the last lap. We've brought Uncle Frank home. Shall I take the lid off?"

"Don't seem any point in delaying things, missy," Dan agreed.

She had to use a knife to cut the rope. The waxen head emerged first. Alice raised her eyebrows. What was she to do with this? There seemed only one solution. She popped it into the coffin, just above Uncle Frank's right shoulder. Dan approved. He then took out Frank's head and carefully placed it back exactly where it should have been. It was a beautiful join. "A tribute to your clean swing," said Alice with heartfelt pride. Both were surprised at how cozy the colonel looked, but neither was surprised to see his eyes full of twinkles. Alice tipped the wax head over so the two heads looked as though they were chatting before her hand sought Dan's and he held it fast. "We should say something," she whispered, "before we put the lid back on."

"I'm no good with words, missy, you know that," murmured Dan, leaning over to settle the hair, "but we could just say "good-bye and Godspeed." I'm not really one for your popish prayers."

"That's perfect," Alice told him, gently serious. "Let's say it together, Dan Skinslicer. Ready?"

"Good-bye and Godspeed, Uncle Frank," they chanted. Hew heard them and wanted to go and join them, but they did not invite him and he did not want to intrude. Alice, still holding on to Dan, touched Frank's eyelids with her fingertips. They closed at once. "Oh!" Alice gave a little jump. "Perhaps that's all we needed to do all along, Dan Skinslicer. Perhaps he could have closed his eyes weeks ago if we'd helped him."

Dan shook his head. "He needed to come home, missy," he said. "He needed to be where he is comfortable." He could see Hew approaching and let go of Alice's hand.

The coffin lid was difficult to get straight, but Alice held it steady while Dan wielded the hammer. It was a noisy business but had a jolly ring to it. In a few moments they were squabbling amicably about the straightness of the nails and whether a special inscription should be put on the coffin explaining the wax head.

But there was no time. As soon as the last nail was hammered home, Father Saunderson summoned four of the Towneley gardeners and they picked up the coffin and disappeared into the dark. There was much scraping as they edged Uncle Frank into his final resting place and slid back the flagstones. The vault was now completely hidden.

Alice felt a curious pang. Uncle Frank had been a more constant companion when dead than he had ever been when alive and she found that she missed him. She leaned against Dan. She knew he understood.

That night, Alice could not sleep. Her bed seemed first too hot, then too cold. When she was small and restless, she used to count the daisies her nurse had embroidered on the bed hangings, but that would not work now. Besides, Alice already knew there were forty-eight and a half, where Nurse had run out of thread. Instead, she got up. Taking a lamp, she left her room and roamed down the long paneled corridor, occasionally peeping into disused bedrooms and frightening the bats. With her candle and lace nightdress, she looked like a wraith, except that she swore when she hit her foot on a doorstop on her way down to the kitchens. She would find something to eat.

The kitchens were not in darkness, for the great fire never went out, and beside it Dan was sitting, his back to the warmth and his head in his hands. Three large wolfhounds were sitting bolt upright watching him.

When Alice approached, the dogs wagged their tails and Dan jumped. "You startled me, missy," he exclaimed.

Alice set her candle down. "I couldn't sleep, Dan Skinslicer," she said. She could feel her heart beating and suddenly the beat was ominous. "Could you not sleep either?" She settled the wolfhounds back into their beds.

"I couldn't," Dan replied shortly. Alice busied herself in the meat safe. She heard Dan's voice behind her. "It was your uncle Frank as reminded me."

She reemerged. "Uncle Frank?"

"Yes. He could only shut his eyes when he was comfortable."

"But aren't you comfortable here, Dan Skinslicer?" Alice forgot about her sore foot. "We could change your room."

"I think you know what I mean, missy."

But Alice didn't want to know what he meant. "Perhaps it's because you need something to do," she said decidedly, and, as if to demonstrate the point, found some bread and began to slice off a mountain of salted lamb. "We'll find you something." •

Dan allowed her to push a plate in front of him. "It's not that." He fiddled with a corner of the bread and made a ball, which he rolled across the table. Alice rolled it back. "I must go," he said, "because in time you will be married to Captain Ffrench."

"But that won't make any difference." Alice pushed the bread ball faster and faster as Dan returned it slower and slower. "What on earth difference could that make?"

"Ah," said Dan. "It will make no difference to you, but it will make a deal of difference to me." He captured the bread ball in his palm.

The shadows in the kitchen were enormous and the dogs yawned and licked their lips. They could smell the lamb and waited expectantly.

"A difference to you, Dan Skinslicer?" Alice looked straight at him now and her voice lost its little-girl chirrup.

Dan threw the bread into a corner and the dogs scuffed over the flags, fighting to get it. Alice hastily threw down more crusts. Both she and Dan were glad of the distraction, but it could not last forever.

"I've never met anybody quite like you, Alice Towneley," said Dan, and his use of her name, the first time he ever had, brought a lump straight into Alice's throat, "and it's not good for me, what you make me feel. The likes of me, see, can never be for the likes of you. We both know that. And Captain Ffrench is a good man who loves you dearly. So I'm happy for you and I'm happy for him. But I can't be happy for me."

Alice made a sound in her throat.

Dan sighed. "Anyway, it doesn't matter. You are better off with him because he thinks you're a saint and I don't. We'd quarrel." He watched a tear drop slowly off the end of Alice's nose. "Oh, don't cry, missy," he said, full of concern. "I didn't mean to make you cry. And anyway, you could never have married me because I've been married already. Johanna is getting a divorce, but even if I was an earl with the grandest coats of arms, that wouldn't be good enough for your type of Catholic."

"But I thought you'd stay here with me. I love you, Dan Skinslicer," Alice sobbed. It was true, it was perfectly true, and nothing would stop her from saying it. "Not in the same way I love Hew, but so much, Dan, so much. If you go, I'll be miserable and nobody will ever tell me off. I think somehow we're meant to be together."

Dan hated her sobs but he shook his head. "In another time, perhaps," he said softly. "One day, in the future, maybe it wouldn't matter that I'm a hangman and you are a lady. But I can't see you making my tea of an evening and asking me how my day went. Can you? Can you honestly?"

Alice wiped her nose and smiled wanly. "No, I suppose not." The dogs sat around her. "But why do you have to be a hangman, Dan Skinslicer? You could be anything—a carpenter or a blacksmith, perhaps, or a butcher, yes, that's right, a butcher! Why didn't I think of it before?"

"I don't want to be a butcher, missy, or any of those other things. I execute people and I'm good at it and,

Lord knows, we need good ones for the poor souls as come to be sent to us."

"You could execute people here!" Alice exclaimed wildly.

Dan got up. "Now you're being fanciful," he said. "When was the last hanging around here?"

Alice began to cry again. "I don't know."

"About a year ago. I asked a man in the village. And there's never been a drawing and quartering. I get more for that. One hanging a year isn't going to keep me going. I need to be back in London, where there's a steady supply. I have my pardon, so nobody will bother me."

"But won't you be lonely? How will I visit you? I have to stay here."

Dan came around to Alice's side of the table and put his huge hands on her shoulders. "Every time I feel lonely I will think of you," he said simply, "and I'll think of how happy—and spoiled—you'll be with Captain Ffrench. Be nice to him, missy." Alice stroked Dan's rough cheek. His voice dropped very low. "I want to ask you something, though," he said. For once in her life, Alice listened hard. "When I am dying," Dan spoke so softly, "I want you to come and close my eyes, just like you did for the colonel. I want you to promise me that if it's possible, and causes you no danger, that the last thing I shall feel on this earth will be your fingers on my eyelids, because, Alice"—he still faltered at her name—"then I'll know for certain sure that despite my sins I'm going to rest in peace."

Alice did not answer. Instead, she climbed off her stool and wound her arms around his neck. They stood, wrapped together, for quite some time, then Dan pulled away, picked up the bag of tools he had left beside the kitchen door, and silently let himself out.

Epilogue

Hew eventually became a Catholic and he and Alice did marry and had lots of children. Neither of them ever forgot Dan, who never married again, and when he caught a fatal fever at the age of seventy, just before the French Revolution, which would, with its scale of executions, have made him a millionaire, Alice answered his call. She traveled to London alone and nursed her old friend patiently through his last months. It was the happiest time Dan had ever known and on days when he felt strong enough, Alice hired a carriage and they picnicked on Kennington Common, reliving old times in the kind of perfect companionship they would never have achieved as man and wife. The day Dan died, it was Alice who closed his eyes, just as he had hoped, and his look of happy peace was so striking that people wondered at it. For a hangman, they said, he must have led a blameless life. Alice took him to Towneley Hall for burial, and she and Hew laid him to rest in the garden with the tools of his trade and a headstone that read:

Dan Skinslicer
Hangman and Jobbing Executioner
HAND ALWAYS STEADY, STEEL ALWAYS SHARP
loved by one who loves him still

Years and years later, Alice and Hew's descendants became confused and believed that Dan was a blood relation, which didn't matter because, in a way, he was.

Mrs. Ffrench came up to live at Towneley, where she found Alice to be a wayward but endearing daughter-in-law, and they became friends. Mabel married Lord Trotting and eventually became the Duchess of Cantankering, which was quite apt, as she remained very cantankerous. Unlike her mother, she never really forgave Alice and couldn't forgive Hew either. When she died, her husband, although far too nice ever to say so, was quite relieved.

As for Ursula, she looked so becoming in the black she wore when pretending that Hew was dead that she never gave it up and when Lady Widdrington died, she made such an impression on the undertaker who organized the funeral that he married her himself. She became very much in demand as a professional mourner and earned a most respectable living. When she died, her husband was genuinely heartbroken and had a large memorial erected to her, giving her age as six years younger than it really was, for no other reason than that he knew it would have pleased her.

Major Slavering lived to a fat old age and suffered badly from gout. Most people said he didn't suffer badly enough and when he died, his funeral was attended only by a couple of stray dogs.

Lord Chief Justice Peckersniff built his house and lived there neither happily nor sadly but in that boring space in between. It was better than his old house, but still not quite big enough to escape his wife. He died in his bed and was supposed to be buried with a handkerchief over his face, but the undertaker forgot, which was a pity.

And what of Uncle Frank's head? In real life, for Uncle Frank did exist, after the head was stolen and brought home, it was not buried, at least not immediately. Since permission could not be got to open his tomb, his head remained in the hatbox and was, for many years, passed around after dinner with the port for everybody to chat to. When he became a little old for that, he was popped behind the paneling of the family chapel before, with the advent of central heating, being packed off to the bank for safekeeping. It was not until 1950 that his head was eventually reunited with his body and, when the tomb was opened in the mid-1970s to see how he was faring, the second head was discovered. Nobody knows to this day to whom the second head belonged. But I believe that if it belonged to anybody, it belonged to Captain Hew Ffrench, lately of Kingston's Light Horse and, as Dan Skinslicer would surely agree, one of the luckiest men in England.